A THRONE FOR SISTERS

(BOOK 1)

MORGAN RICE

AN OATH OF BROTHERS (Book #14)
A DREAM OF MORTALS (Book #15)
A JOUST OF KNIGHTS (Book #16)
THE GIFT OF BATTLE (Book #17)

THE SURVIVAL TRILOGY
ARENA ONE: SLAVERSUNNERS (Book #1)
ARENA TWO (Book #2)
ARENA THREE (Book #3)

VAMPIRE, FALLEN
BEFORE DAWN (Book #1)

THE VAMPIRE JOURNALS
TURNED (Book #1)
LOVED (Book #2)
BETRAYED (Book #3)
DESTINED (Book #4)
DESIRED (Book #5)
BETROTHED (Book #6)
VOWED (Book #7)
FOUND (Book #8)
RESURRECTED (Book #9)
CRAVED (Book #10)
FATED (Book #11)
OBSESSED (Book #12)

CHAPTER ONE

Of all the things to hate in the House of the Unclaimed, the grinding wheel was the one Sophia dreaded most. She groaned as she pushed against an arm connected to the giant post that disappeared into the floor, while around her, the other orphans shoved against theirs. She ached and sweated as she pushed at it, her red hair matting with the work, her rough gray dress staining further with the sweat. Her dress was shorter than she wanted now, riding up with every stride to show the tattoo on her calf in the shape of a mask, marking her as what she was: an orphan, an owned thing.

The other girls there had things even worse. At seventeen, Sophia was at least one of the oldest and largest of them. The only person older in the room was Sister O'Venn. The nun of the Masked Goddess wore the jet black habit of her order, along with a lace mask that every orphan quickly learned she could see through, down to the smallest detail of failure. The sister held the leather strap that she used to dole out punishment, flexing it between her hands while she droned on in the background, uttering the words of the *Book of Masks*, homilies about the need to perfect abandoned souls such as them.

"In this place, you learn to be useful," she intoned. "In this place, you learn to be valuable, as you were not to whatever fallen women gave birth to you. The Masked Goddess tells us that we must shape our place in the world through our efforts, and today your efforts turn the querns that grind the corn and—pay attention, Sophia!"

Sophia flinched as she felt the impact of her belt as it cracked out. She gritted her teeth. How many times had the sisters beaten her in her life? For doing the wrong thing, or for not doing the right thing quickly enough? For being pretty enough that it constituted a sin in and of itself? For having the flame red hair of a troublemaker?

If only they knew about her talent. She shuddered to think of it. For then, they would have beaten her to death.

"Are you ignoring me, you stupid girl?" the nun demanded. She struck out again, and again. "Kneel facing the wall, all of you!"

1

That was the worst part: it didn't *matter* if you did everything right. The sisters would beat everyone for the failings of one girl.

"You need to be reminded," Sister O'Venn snapped, as Sophia heard a girl cry out, "of what you are. Of *where* you are." Another girl whimpered as the leather strap struck flesh. "You are the children no one wanted. You are the property of the Masked Goddess, given a home through her grace."

She made her way around the room, and Sophia knew she would be last. The idea was to make her feel guilt for the pain of the others, and give them time to hate her for bringing this on them, before she got her beating.

The beating she was kneeling there waiting for.

When she could just leave.

That thought came to Sophia so unbidden that she had to check it wasn't some kind of sending from her younger sister, or that she hadn't picked it up from one of the others. That was the problem with a talent like hers: it came when it wanted, not when called. Yet it seemed that the thought really was hers—and more than that, it was true.

Better to risk death than to stay here one more day.

Of course, if she dared to walk away, the punishment would be worse. They always found a way to make it worse. Sophia had seen girls who had stolen or fought back starved for days, forced to keep kneeling, beaten when they tried to sleep.

But she didn't care anymore. Something inside her had crossed a line. The fear couldn't touch her, because it was swamped in the fear of what would happen soon anyway.

After all, she turned seventeen today.

She was now old enough to repay her debt of years of "care" at the hands of the nuns—to be indentured and sold like livestock. Sophia knew what happened to orphans who came of age. Compared to that, no beating mattered.

She had been turning it over in her mind for weeks, in fact. Dreading this day, her birthday.

And now it had arrived.

To her own shock, Sophia acted. She stood smoothly, looked around. The nun's attention was on another girl, whipping her savagely, so it was but the work of a moment to slip over to the door in silence. Probably even the other girls didn't notice, or if they did, they were too frightened to say anything.

Sophia stepped out into one of the plain white corridors of the orphanage, moving quietly, walking away from the workroom.

There were other nuns out there, but so long as she moved with purpose, it might be enough to keep them from stopping her.

What had she just done?

Sophia kept walking through the House of the Unclaimed in a daze, barely able to believe that she was actually doing this. There were reasons they didn't bother locking the front gates. The city beyond, just outside its gates, was a rough place—and rougher still for those who had started life as an orphan. Ashton had every city's thieves and thugs—yet it also contained the hunters who recaptured the indentured who ran and the free folk who would spit on her simply for what she was.

Then there was her sister. Kate was only fifteen. Sophia didn't want to drag her into something worse. Kate was tough, tougher even than her, yet she was still Sophia's little sister.

Sophia wandered down toward the cloisters and the courtyard where they mixed with the boys from the orphanage next door, trying to work out where her sister would be. She couldn't leave without her.

She was almost there when she heard a girl cry out.

Sophia headed toward the sound, half suspecting that her little sister had gotten herself into another fight. When she reached the yard, though, she didn't find Kate at the center of a brawling mob, but another girl instead. This one was even younger, perhaps in her thirteenth year, and was being pushed and slapped by three boys who must have been almost old enough to sell off into apprenticeships or the army.

"Stop that!" Sophia cried out, surprising herself as much as she seemed to surprise the boys there. Normally the rule was that you walked past whatever was happening in the orphanage. You stayed quiet and remembered your place. Now, though, she stepped forward.

"Leave her be."

The boys paused, but only to stare at her.

The oldest set his eyes upon her with a malicious grin.

"Well, well, boys," he said, "looks like we have another one who isn't where she should be."

He had blunt features and the kind of dead look in his eyes that only came from years in the House of the Unclaimed.

He stepped forward, and before she could react, he grabbed Sophia's arm. She went to slap him, but he was too quick, and he shoved her to the floor. It was in moments like this that Sophia wished she had her younger sister's fighting skills, her ability to

3

summon an instant brutality that Sophia, for all her cunning, just wasn't capable of.

Going to be sold as a whore anyway... might as well have my turn.

Sophia was startled to hear his thoughts. These had an almost greasy feel to them, and she knew they were his. Her panic welled up.

She started to struggle, but he pinned her arms easily.

There was only one thing she could do. She screwed up her concentration, calling on her talent, hoping that this time it would work for her.

Kate, she sent, *the courtyard! Help me!*

*

"More elegantly, Kate!" the nun called. "More *elegantly*!"

Kate didn't have a lot of time for elegance, but still, she made the effort as she poured water into a goblet held by the sister. Sister Yvaine regarded her critically from beneath her mask.

"No, you still haven't got it. And I know you're not clumsy, girl. I've seen you turning cartwheels in the yard."

She hadn't punished Kate for it, though, which suggested that Sister Yvaine wasn't one of the worst of them. Kate tried again, her hand trembling.

She and the other girls with her were supposed to be learning to serve elegantly at noble tables, but the truth was that Kate wasn't built for it. She was too short and too tightly muscled for the kind of graceful femininity the nuns had in mind. There was a reason she kept her red hair hacked short. In the ideal world, where she was free to choose, she yearned for an apprenticeship with a smith or perhaps one of the groups of players who worked in the city—or perhaps even a chance to go into the army as the boys did. This graceful pouring was the kind of lesson her big sister, with her dream of aristocracy, would have enjoyed—not her.

As if the thought summoned her, Kate suddenly snapped to as she heard her sister's voice in her mind. She wondered, though; their talent wasn't always that reliable.

But then it came again, and there, too, was the feeling behind it.

Kate, the courtyard! Help me!

Kate could feel the fear there.

She stepped away from the nun sharply, involuntarily, and in so doing she spilled her jug of water across the stone of the floor.

"I'm sorry," she said. "I need to go."

4

Sister Yvaine was still staring at the water.

"Kate, clean that up at once!"

But Kate was already running. She would probably find herself beaten for it later, but she'd been beaten before. It didn't mean anything. Helping the one person in the world she cared about did.

She ran through the orphanage. She knew the way, because she'd learned every twist and turn of the place in the years since that awful night they dropped her here. She also, late at night, sneaked out from the ceaseless snoring and stench of the dormitory when she could, enjoying the place in the blackness when she was the only one up, when the tolling of the city's bells was the only sound, and learning the feel of every nook in its walls. She sensed she would need it one day.

And now she did.

Kate could hear the sound of her sister, fighting and calling for help. On instinct, she ducked into a room, grabbing a poker from the fire grate and continuing on. What she would do with it, she didn't know.

She burst into the courtyard, and her heart fell to see her sister being pinned down by two boys while another fumbled with her dress.

Kate knew exactly what to do.

A primal rage overcame her, one she could not control if she wished, and Kate rushed forward with a roar, swinging the poker at the first boy's head. He turned as Kate struck, so it didn't hit him as well as she wanted, but it was still enough to send him sprawling, clutching at the spot she'd hit.

She lashed out at another, catching him across the knee as he stood, making him tumble. She struck the third in the stomach, until he keeled over.

She kept hitting, not wanting to give the boys any time to recover. She'd been in plenty of fights in her years at the orphanage, and she knew that she couldn't rely on size or strength. Fury was the only thing she had to carry her through. And thankfully, Kate had plenty of that.

She struck and she struck, until the boys fell back. They might have been prepared to join the army, but the Masked Brothers on their side didn't teach them to fight. That would have made them too hard to control. Kate struck one of the boys in the face, then spun back to hit another's elbow with a crack of iron on bone.

"Stand up," she said to her sister, holding out her hand. "Stand *up*!"

Her sister stood numbly, taking Kate's hand as though she were the younger sister for once.

Kate set off running, and her sister ran with her. Sophia appeared to come back to herself as they ran, some of the old certainty seeming to return as they raced along the corridors of the orphanage.

Behind them, Kate could hear shouting, from boys or sisters or both. She didn't care. She knew there was no way but out.

"We can't go back," Sophia said. "We have to leave the orphanage."

Kate nodded. Something like this wouldn't earn just a beating as punishment. But then Kate remembered.

"Then we go," Kate replied, running. "First I just need to—"

"No," Sophia said. "There's no time. Leave everything. We need to *go*."

Kate shook her head. There were some things she couldn't leave behind.

So instead, she raced in the direction of her dormitory, keeping hold of Sophia's arm so that she would follow.

The dormitory was a bleak place, with beds that were little more than wooden slats sticking out from the wall like shelves. Kate wasn't stupid enough to put anything that mattered in the small chest at the foot of her bed, where anyone could steal it. Instead, she went to a crack between two floorboards, worrying at it with her fingers until one lifted.

"Kate," Sophia huffed and puffed, catching her breath, "there's no time."

Kate shook her head.

"I won't leave it behind."

Sophia had to know what she'd come for; the one memento she had from that night, from their old life.

Finally, Kate's finger's fastened around metal, and she lifted the locket clear to shine in the dim light.

When she was a child, she'd been sure that it was real gold; a fortune waiting to be spent. As she'd gotten older, she'd come to see that it was some cheaper alloy, but by then, it had come to be worth far more than gold to her anyway. The miniature inside, of a woman smiling while a man had his hand on her shoulder, was the closest thing to a memory of her parents she had.

Kate normally didn't wear it for fear that one of the other children, or the nuns, would take it from her. Now, she tucked it inside her dress.

"Let's go," she said.

6

They ran for the door to the orphanage, supposedly always open because the Masked Goddess had found doors closed to her when she visited the world and had condemned those within. Kate and Sophia ran down the twists and turns of the corridors, coming out to the hallway, looking around for any pursuers.

Kate could hear them, but right then, there was only the usual sister beside the door: a fat woman who moved to block the way even as the two of them approached. Kate flushed red as she immediately recalled all the years of beatings she'd taken by her hands.

"There you are," she said in a stern tone. "You've both been very disobedient, and——"

Kate didn't pause; she hit her in the stomach with the poker, hard enough to double her up. Right then, she wished it were one of the elegant swords that courtiers wore, or maybe an axe. As it was, she had to settle for merely stunning the woman long enough for her and Sophia to run past.

But then, as Kate passed through the doors, she stopped.

"Kate!" Sophia yelled, panic in her voice. "Let's go! What are you doing?!"

But Kate couldn't control it. Even with the shouts of those in hot pursuit. Even knowing it was risking both of their freedom.

She took two steps forward, raised the poker high, and smashed the nun again and again across her back.

The nun grunted and cried with each blow, and each sound was music to Kate's ears.

"Kate!" Sophia pleaded, on the verge of tears.

Kate stared at the nun for a long time, too long, needing to ingrain that picture of vengeance, of justice, into her mind. It would sustain her, she knew, for whatever horrific beatings might follow.

Then she turned and burst out with her sister from the House of the Unclaimed, like two fugitives from a sinking ship. The stink and noise and bustle of the city hit Kate, but this time she didn't slow.

She held her sister's hand and ran.

And ran.

And ran.

And despite it all, she took a deep breath and smiled wide.

However short it might be, they had found freedom.

CHAPTER TWO

Sophia had never been so afraid, but at the same time, she had never felt so alive, or so free. As she ran through the city with her sister, she heard Kate whoop with the excitement of it, and it both set her at ease and terrified her. It made this too real. Their life would never be the same again.

"Quiet," Sophia insisted. "You'll bring them down on us."

"They're coming anyway," her sister replied. "We might as well enjoy it."

As if to emphasize the point, she dodged around a horse, snatched an apple from a cart, and ran across Ashton's cobbles.

The city was bustling with the market that came to it every Sixthday, and Sophia looked around, startled at all the sights and sounds and smells. If it weren't for the market, she'd have no idea what day it was. In the House of the Unclaimed, those things didn't matter, only the endless cycles of prayer and work, punishment and rote learning.

Run faster, her sister sent.

The sound of whistles and cries somewhere behind them spurred her on to new speed. Sophia led the way down an alley, then struggled to follow as Kate scrambled over a wall. Her sister, for all her impetuosity, was too quick, like a solid, coiled muscle waiting to spring.

Sophia barely managed to clamber over as more whistles sounded, and as she neared the top, Kate's strong hand was waiting for her, as always. Even in this, she realized, they were so different: Kate's hand was rough, calloused, muscular, while Sophia's fingers were long and smooth and delicate.

Two sides of the same coin, their mother used to say.

"They've summoned the watchmen," Kate called out in disbelief, as if that somehow wasn't playing fair.

"What did you expect?" Sophia replied. "We're running away before they can sell us off."

Kate led the way down narrow cobblestone steps, then toward an open space thronging with people. Sophia forced herself to slow as they approached the city's market, holding onto Kate's forearm to keep her from running.

We'll blend in more if we aren't running, Sophia sent, too out of breath to speak.

Kate didn't look certain, but she still matched Sophia's pace.

They walked slowly, brushing past people who stepped aside, obviously unwilling to risk contact with anyone as lowborn as them. Perhaps they thought that the two were released for some errand.

Sophia forced herself to look as though she were just browsing while they used the crowd for camouflage. She looked around, to the clock tower above the temple of the Masked Goddess, at the various stalls, and the glass-fronted shops beyond them. There was a group of players in one corner of the square, acting out one of the traditional tales in elaborate costumes while one of the censors looked on from the edge of the surrounding crowd. There was a recruiter for the army standing on a box, trying to recruit troops for the newest war to take hold of this city, a looming battle across the Knife-Water Channel.

Sophia saw her sister eyeing the recruiter, and pulled her back.

No, Sophia sent. *That's not for you.*

Kate was about to reply when suddenly the shouts began again behind them.

They both took off.

Sophia knew that no one would help them now. This was Ashton, which meant that she and Kate were the ones in the wrong here. No one would try to help two runaways.

In fact, as she looked up, Sophia saw someone start to move into their way, to block them. No one would let two orphans get away from what they owed, from what they were.

Hands grabbed for them, and now they had to fight their way through. Sophia slapped away a hand from her shoulder, while Kate jabbed viciously with her stolen poker.

A gap opened up in front of them, and Sophia saw her sister running for a section of abandoned wooden scaffolding beside a stone wall, where builders must have been trying to straighten a façade.

More climbing? Sophia sent.

They won't follow us, her sister shot back.

Which was probably true, if only because the chasing pack of ordinary people wouldn't risk their lives like that. Sophia dreaded it, though. Yet she couldn't think of any better ideas right then.

Her shaking hands closed around the wooden slats of the scaffolding, and she started to climb.

In a matter of moments, her arms started to ache, but by then it was either keep going or fall, and even if there hadn't been the

9

cobbles below, Sophia didn't want to fall with most of a mob chasing after her.

Kate was already waiting at the top, still grinning as if the whole thing were some game. Her hand was there again, and she pulled Sophia up, and then they were running again—this time on rooftops.

Kate led the way to a gap leading to another roof, hopping into the thatch as if she didn't care about the risk of going through. Sophia followed her, biting back the urge to cry out as she nearly slipped, then leaping with her sister onto a low section where a dozen chimneys belched out smoke from a kiln below.

Kate tried to run again, but Sophia, sensing an opportunity, grabbed her and yanked her down into the thatch, hidden amongst the stacks.

Wait, she sent.

To her amazement, Kate didn't argue. She looked about as they huddled down in the flat section of roof, ignoring the heat coming up from the fires below, and she must have realized how hidden they were. The smoke blurred most of what was around them, putting them in a fog, further hiding them. It was like a second city up here, with lines of clothes, flags, and pennants providing all the cover they could want. If they stayed still, no one could possibly spot them here. Nor would anyone else be foolish enough to risk treading on the thatch.

Sophia looked about. It was peaceful up here in its own way. There were spots where the houses were close enough that neighbors could reach out to touch one another, and further along, Sophie saw a chamber pot being emptied into the street. She'd never had a chance to see the city from this angle, the towers of the clergy and the shot makers, the clock keepers and the wise men rising up over the rest of it, the palace sitting in its own ring of walls like some shining carbuncle on the skin of the rest.

She hunched down there with her sister, her arms wrapped around Kate, and waited for the sounds of pursuit to pass below.

Maybe, just maybe, they'd find a way out.

CHAPTER THREE

Morning faded into afternoon before Sophia and Kate dared to creep out of their hiding place. As Sophia had thought, no one had dared clamber up onto the rooftops to search for them, and while the sounds of pursuit had come close, they'd never quite come close enough.

Now, they seemed to have faded entirely.

Kate peeked out and looked down at the city below. The morning's bustle was gone, replaced by a more relaxed pace and crowd.

"We need to get down from here," Sophia whispered to her sister.

Kate nodded. "I'm starving."

Sophia could understand that. Their stolen apple was long gone, and hunger was starting to gnaw at her stomach, too.

They lowered themselves to street level, and Sophia found herself looking around as they did. Even though the sounds of people hunting for them had gone, a part of her was convinced that someone would leap out at them the moment their feet touched the ground.

They picked their way through the streets, trying to keep out of sight as much as they could. It was impossible to avoid people in Ashton, though, because there were simply so many of them. The nuns hadn't bothered to teach them much about the shape of the world, but Sophia had heard that there were bigger cities beyond the Merchant States.

Right then, it was hard to believe it. There were people everywhere she looked, even though most of the city's population had to be inside, hard at work, by now. There were children playing on the street, women walking to and from markets and shops, workmen carrying tools and ladders. There were taverns and playhouses, shops selling coffee from the newly discovered lands past the Mirror Ocean, cafes where people seemed to be almost as interested in talking as in eating. She could hardly believe to see people laughing, happy, so carefree, doing nothing but idling the time and enjoying themselves. She could hardly believe that such a world could even exist. It was a shocking contrast to the enforced quiet and obedience of the orphanage.

There's so much, Sophia sent to her sister, eyeing the food stalls everywhere, feeling her stomach pain grow with each passing smell.

Kate was looking around it all with a practical eye. She picked one of the cafes, moving up toward it cautiously while people outside laughed at a would-be philosopher trying to argue over how much of the world it was possible to really know.

"You'd have an easier time if you weren't drunk," one of them heckled.

Another turned toward Sophia and Kate as they approached. The hostility there was palpable.

"We don't want your sort here," he sneered. "Get out!"

The sheer anger of it was more than Sophia had expected. Still, she shuffled back to the street, pulling Kate with her so that her sister wouldn't do anything they'd regret. She might have dropped her poker somewhere in running from the mob, but she certainly had a look that said she wanted to hit something.

They had no choice, then: they would have to steal their food. Sophia had hoped that someone might show them charity. Yet that wasn't the way the world worked, she knew.

It was time to use their talents, they both realized, nodding to each silently at the same time. They stood on opposite sides of an alley and both watched and waited as a baker worked. Sophia waited until the baker could read her thoughts, and then told her what she wanted her to hear.

Oh no, the baker thought. *The rolls. How could I forget them inside?*

Barely had the baker had the thought than Sophia and Kate burst into action, rushing forward the second the woman turned her back to go back inside for the rolls. They moved quickly, each snatching an armful of cakes, enough to fill their bellies almost to bursting.

They both ducked behind an alley and chewed ravenously. Soon, Sophia felt her belly full, a strange and pleasant sensation, and one she'd never had. The House of the Unclaimed didn't believe in feeding its charges more than the bare minimum.

Now she laughed as Kate attempted to shove an entire pastry into her mouth.

What? her sister demanded.

It's just good to see you happy, Sophia sent back.

She wasn't sure how long that happiness would last. She kept an eye out with every step for the hunters who might be after them. The orphanage wouldn't want to put more effort into reclaiming them than their indentures were worth, but who could tell when it came to the vindictiveness of the nuns? At the very least, they would have to keep clear of the watchmen, and not just because they'd escaped.

Thieves, after all, were hanged in Ashton.

We need to stop looking like runaway orphans or we'll never be able to walk through the city without people staring and trying to catch us.

Sophia looked over at her sister, surprised by the thought.

You want to steal clothes? Sophia sent back.

Kate nodded.

That thought brought an extra note of fear and yet Sophia knew her sister, ever practical, was right.

They both stood at the same time, stuffing the extra cakes in their waists. Sophia was looking about for clothes, when she felt Kate touch her arm. She followed her gaze and saw it: a clothesline, high up on a roof. It was unguarded.

Of course it would be, she realized with relief. *Who, after all, would guard a clothesline?*

Even so, Sophia could feel her heart pounding as they clambered up onto another roof. They both paused, looked about, then reeled in the line the way a fisherman might have pulled in a line of fish.

Sophia stole an outer dress of green wool, along with a cream underdress that was probably the kind of thing a farmer's wife might wear, but was still impossibly rich to her. To her surprise, her sister picked out an undershirt, breeches, and doublet, which left her looking more like a spike-haired boy than the girl she was.

"Kate," Sophia complained. "You can't run around looking like that!"

Kate shrugged. "Neither of us is supposed to look like this. I might as well be comfortable."

There was a kind of truth in that. The sumptuary laws were clear about what each grade of society could and couldn't wear, the unclaimed and the indentured. Here they were, breaking more laws, tossing aside their rags, the only thing they were allowed to wear, and dressing better than they were.

"All right," Sophia said. "I won't argue. Besides, maybe it will throw off anyone who is looking for two girls," she said with a laugh.

"I do *not* look like a boy," Kate snapped back in obvious indignation.

Sophia smiled at that. They salvaged their cakes, stuffed them in their new pockets, and together, they were off.

The next part was harder to smile about; there remained so many things they needed to do if they wanted to actually survive. They had to find shelter, for one thing, and then work out what they were going to do, where they were going to go.

One step at a time, she reminded herself.

They scrambled back down to the streets, and this time Sophia led the way, trying to find a route through the poorer section of the city, still too close to the orphanage for her tastes.

She saw a string of burnt out houses ahead, obviously not recovered from one of the fires that sometimes swept through the city when the river was low. It would be a dangerous place to rest.

Even so, Sophia headed for them.

Kate gave her a wondering, skeptical look.

Sophia shrugged.

Dangerous is better than nothing at all, she sent.

They approached cautiously, and just as Sophia stuck her head around the corner, she was startled as a pair of figures rose up out of the wreckage. They appeared so soot-blackened by staying in the charred remains that for a moment Sophia thought they'd been in the fire.

"Geddout! Leave our patch alone!"

One of them rushed at Sophia, and she shrieked as she took an involuntary step back. Kate looked as though she might fight, but then the other figure there pulled a dagger that shone far brighter than anything else there.

"This is our claim! Pick your own ruin, or I'll bleed you."

The sisters ran then, putting as much distance between them and the house as they could. With every step, Sophia was sure that she could hear the footsteps of knife-wielding thugs, or watchmen, or the nuns, somewhere behind them.

They walked until their legs hurt and the afternoon grew far too dark. At least they took solace that, with every step, they were one step farther from the orphanage.

Finally, they approached a slightly better part of town. For some reason, Kate's face brightened at the sight of it.

"What is it?" Sophia asked.

"The penny library," her sister replied. "We can slip in there. I sneak away sometimes, when the sisters send us on errands, and the librarian lets me in even though I don't have the penny to pay."

Sophia didn't hold much hope of finding help there, but the truth was that she didn't have any better ideas. She let Kate lead her, and they headed for a busy space where moneylenders mixed with advocates and there were even a few carriages mixed in with the normal horses and pedestrians.

The library was one of the larger buildings there. Sophia knew the story: that one of the nobles of the city had decided to educate the poor and left a portion of his fortune to build the kind of library that most just kept locked away in their country homes. Of course, charging a penny a visit still meant that the poorest couldn't visit. Sophia had never had a penny. The nuns saw no reason to give their charges money.

She and Kate approached the entrance, and she saw an aging man sitting there, soft looking in slightly worn clothes, obviously as much a guard as a librarian. To Sophia's surprise, he smiled as they approached. Sophia had never seen anyone happy to see her sister before.

"Young Kate," he said. "It has been a while since you have been here. And you've brought a friend. Go through, go through. I will not stand in the way of knowledge. Earl Varrish's son may have put a penny tax on knowledge, but the old earl never believed in it."

He seemed genuine about it, but Kate was already shaking her head.

"That's not what we need, Geoffrey," Kate said. "My sister and I...we ran away from the orphanage."

Sophia caught the shock on the older man's face.

"No," he said. "No, you must not do such a foolish thing."

"It's done," Sophia said.

"Then you cannot be here," Geoffrey insisted. "If the watch come, and they find you here with me, they may assume that I had some role in this."

Sophia would have left then, but it seemed that Kate still wanted to try.

"Please, Geoffrey," Kate said. "I need—"

"You need to go back," Geoffrey said. "Beg forgiveness. I have pity for your situation, but it *is* the situation fate has handed you. Go back before the watch catch you. I cannot help you. I may even be flogged for not alerting the watch that I saw you. That is all the kindness I can give you."

His voice was harsh, and yet Sophia could see the kindness in his eyes, and that it pained him to say the words. Almost as if he were battling himself, as if he were putting on a show of being harsh only to drive home his point.

Even so, Kate looked crushed. Sophia hated to see her sister that way.

Sophia pulled her back, away from the library.

As they walked, Kate, head down, finally spoke.

"What now?" she asked.

The truth was that Sophia didn't have an answer.

They kept walking, but by now, she was exhausted from walking so long. It was starting to rain, too, in that steady way that suggested it wouldn't stop soon. Few places did rain the way Ashton did.

Sophia found herself gravitating down the sloped cobblestone streets toward the river that ran through the city. Sophia wasn't sure what she hoped to find there, among the barges and the flat-bottomed punts. She doubted that wharf hands or whores were likely to be of any help to them, and those seemed to be the main things this part of the city held. But at least it was a destination. If nothing else, they could find a place to hide by its shores and watch the peaceful sailing of the ships, and dream of other places.

Eventually, Sophia spotted a shallow overhang near one of the city's many bridges. She approached. She reeled from the stench, as did Kate, and the infestation of rats. But her tiredness made even the meanest scrap of shelter seem like a palace. They had to get out of the rain. They had to get out of sight. And right then, what else was there? They had to find a spot where no one else, even vagrants, dared to go. And this was it.

"Here?" Kate asked, in disgust. "Couldn't we go back to the chimney?"

Sophia shook her head. She doubted that they would be able to find it again, and even if they could, it would be where any hunters would start to look. This was the best place they were going to find before the rain got worse and before night fell.

She settled down and tried to hide her tears for her sister's sake.

Slowly, reluctantly, Kate sat down beside her, clutching her arms to her knees and rocking herself, as if to shut out the cruelty and barbarism and hopelessness of the world.

CHAPTER FOUR

In Kate's dreams, her parents were still alive, and she was happy. Whenever she dreamed, it seemed that they were there, although the faces weren't memories so much as constructed things, with only the locket to guide them. Kate hadn't been old enough for more when it all changed.

She was in a house somewhere in the countryside, where the view from the leaded windows took in orchards and fields. Kate dreamed the warmth of the sun on her skin, the gentle breeze that ruffled through the leaves outside.

The next part never seemed to make sense. She didn't know enough of the details, or she hadn't remembered them right. She tried to force her dream to give her the whole story of what had happened, but it gave her fragments instead:

An open window, with stars outside. Her sister's hand, Sophia's voice in her head, telling her to hide. Looking for their parents through the maze of the house...

Hiding through the house in the dark. Hearing the sounds of someone moving about there. There was light beyond, even though it was night outside. She felt she was close, on the verge of discovering what finally happened to their parents that night. The light from the window started to grow brighter, and brighter, and—

"Wake up," Sophia said, shaking her. "You're dreaming, Kate."

Kate's eyes flickered open resentfully. Dreams were always so much better than the world she lived in.

She squinted at the light. Impossibly, morning had arrived. Her first day ever sleeping a full night outside the stench and screams of the orphanage's walls, her first morning ever waking up somewhere, anywhere, else. Even in a dank place like this, she was elated.

She noticed not just the difference from the failing afternoon light; it was the way the river in front of them had sprung into life with the barges and boats hurrying to make the most distance upriver they could. Some moved with small sails, others with poles pushing them or horses towing them from the side of the river.

Around them, Kate could hear the rest of the city waking up. The bells of the temple were sounding the hour, while in between, she could hear the chatter of a whole city's worth of people making their way to work, or setting off on other journeys. Today was

Firstday, a good day to begin things. Maybe that would mean good luck for her and Sophia, too.

"I keep having the same dream," Kate said. "I keep dreaming about... about that night."

They always seemed to stop short of calling it more than that. It was strange, when they could probably communicate more directly than anyone else in the city, that she and Sophia still hesitated talking around this one thing.

Sophia's expression darkened, and Kate immediately felt bad about that.

"I dream about it too, sometimes," Sophia admitted sadly.

Kate turned to her, focused. Her sister had to know. She'd been older, she would have seen more.

"You *know* what happened, don't you?" Kate asked. "You know what happened with our parents."

It was more of a statement than a question.

Kate scanned her sister's face for answers, and she saw it, just a flicker, something she was hiding.

Sophia shook her head.

"There are some things it's better not to think about. We need to focus on what happens next, not on the past."

It wasn't exactly a satisfying answer, but it was no more than Kate had expected. Sophia wouldn't talk about what happened the night their parents left. She never wanted to discuss it, and even Kate had to admit to feelings of unease every time she thought about it. Besides, in the House of the Unclaimed, they didn't like it when orphans tried to talk about the past. They called it ungrateful, and it was just one more thing worthy of punishment.

Kate kicked a rat off of her foot and sat up straighter, looking around.

"We can't stay where we are," she said.

Sophia nodded.

"We'll die if we stay here on the streets."

That was a hard thought, but it was probably true, as well. There were so many ways to die in the streets of this city. Cold and hunger were just the start of the list. With the street gangs, the watch, disease, and all the other risks out here, even the orphanage started to look safe.

Not that Kate would ever go back. She would burn it to the ground before she stepped back through its doors. Maybe one day she would burn it to the ground anyway. She smiled at that.

Feeling a hunger pain, Kate pulled out the last of her cake and began to wolf it down. Then she remembered her sister. She tore off half and handed it to her.

Sophia looked at her hopefully, but with guilt.

"It's okay," Kate lied. "I have another in my dress."

Sophia took it reluctantly. Kate sensed her sister knew she was lying, but was too hungry to deny herself. Yet their connection was so close, Kate could feel her sister's hunger, and Kate could never allow herself to be happy if her sister was not.

They both finally crept out of their hiding place.

"So, big sister," Kate asked, "any ideas?"

Sophie sighed sadly and shook her head.

"Well, I'm starving," Kate said. "It will be better to think on a full belly."

Sophia nodded in agreement, and they both headed back toward the main streets.

They soon found a target—a different baker—and stole breakfast the way they'd stolen their last meal. As they ducked into an alley and gorged themselves, it was tempting to think that they might live the rest of their lives like that, using their shared talent to take what they needed when no one was paying attention. But Kate knew it couldn't work like that. Nothing good lasted forever.

Kate looked out at the bustle of the city before her. It was overwhelming. And its streets seemed to stretch forever.

"If we can't stay out on the street," she said, "what do we do? Where do we go?"

Sophia hesitated for a moment, looking as though she was as unsure as Kate was.

"I don't know," she admitted.

"Well, what *can* we do?" Kate asked.

It didn't seem like as long a list as it should have been. The truth was that orphans like them didn't get options in their lives. They were prepared for lives where they would be indentured as apprentices or servants, soldiers, or worse. There was no real expectation that they would ever be free, because even those genuinely looking for an apprentice would only pay a pittance; not enough to ever pay off their debt.

And the truth was that Kate had little patience for sewing or cooking, etiquette or haberdashery.

"We could find some trader and try to apprentice ourselves," Kate suggested.

Sophia shook her head.

"Even if we could find one willing to take us on, they would want to hear from our families beforehand. When we couldn't produce a father to vouch for us, they would know what we were."

Kate had to admit that her sister had a point.

"Well then, we could sign on as barge hands, and see the rest of the country."

Even as she said it, she knew that was probably just as ludicrous as her first idea. A barge captain would still ask questions, and probably any hunters of escaped orphans would watch the barges for those trying to escape. They certainly couldn't rely on someone else to help them, not after what had happened in the library, with the only man in this city she had considered a friend.

What a naïve fool she had been.

Sophia seemed to get the enormity of what faced them as well. She was looking away with a wistful expression on her face.

"If you could do anything," Sophia asked, "if you could go anywhere, where would you go?"

Kate hadn't thought about it in those terms.

"I don't know," she said. "I mean, I never thought past just surviving the day."

Sophia fell silent for a long time. Kate could feel her thinking.

Finally, Sophia spoke.

"If we try to do anything normal, there are going to be just as many obstacles as if we shoot for the biggest things in the world. Maybe even more, because people *expect* people like us to settle for less. So what do you want, more than anything?"

Kate thought about that.

"I want to find our parents," Kate said, realizing it as she spoke it.

She could feel the flash of pain that ran through Sophia with those words.

"Our parents are dead," Sophia said. She sounded so certain that Kate wanted to ask her again what had happened all those years ago. "I'm sorry, Kate. That wasn't what I meant."

Kate sighed bitterly.

"I don't want anyone to control what I do again," Kate said, picking the thing that she wanted almost as much as their parents' return. "I want to be free, *truly* free."

"I want that as well," Sophia said. "But there are very few truly *free* people in this city. The only ones really are…"

She looked out across the city and, following her gaze, Kate could see that she was looking out toward the palace, with its shining marble and its gilt decorations.

20

Kate could feel what she was thinking.

"I don't think being a servant at the palace would make you free," Kate said.

"I wasn't thinking about being a servant," Sophia snapped. "What if…what if we could just walk in there and be one of them? What if we could persuade them all that we were? What if we could marry some rich man, have connections at court?"

Kate didn't laugh, but only because she could tell how serious her sister was about the whole idea. If she could have anything in the world, the last thing Kate would want would be to walk into the palace and become a great lady, to marry some man who told her what to do.

"I don't want to depend on anyone else for my freedom," Kate said. "The world has taught us one thing, and one thing only: we must depend on ourselves. *Only* on ourselves. That way we can control everything that happens to us. And we don't have to trust anyone. We have to learn to take care of ourselves. To sustain ourselves. To live off the land. To learn to hunt. To farm. Anything where we don't rely on anyone else. And we have to amass great weapons and become great fighters, so if anyone comes to take what is ours, we can kill them."

And suddenly, Kate realized.

"We need to leave this city," she urged her sister. "It's filled with dangers for us. We need to live out beyond the city, in the country, where few people live and where no one will be able to harm us."

The more she spoke about it, the more she realized that it was the right thing to do. It was her dream. Right then, Kate wanted nothing more than to run for the gates of the city, out into the open spaces beyond.

"And when we learn to fight," Kate added, "when we become bigger and stronger and have the finest swords and crossbows and daggers, we will come back here and kill everyone who hurt us in the orphanage."

She felt Sophia's hands on her shoulder.

"You can't talk like that, Kate. You can't just talk about killing people like it's nothing."

"It's not nothing," Kate spat. "It's what they *deserve*."

Sophia shook her head.

"That is primitive," Sophia said. "There are better ways to survive. And better ways to get revenge. Besides, I don't want to just *survive*, like some peasant in the woods. What is the point of life then? I want to *live*."

Kate wasn't sure about that, but she didn't say anything.

They walked on in silence for a little way, and Kate guessed that Sophia was as caught up in her dream as Kate was. They walked along streets filled with people who seemed to know what they were doing with their lives, who seemed filled with a sense of purpose, and to Kate, it was unfair that it should be so easy for them. Then again, maybe it wasn't. Maybe they had as little choice as she or Sophia would have had if they'd stayed in the orphanage.

Ahead, the city sprawled beyond gates that had probably been there for hundreds of years. The space beyond was filled with houses now, pushed right up against the walls in a way that probably made them useless. There was a wide open space beyond, though, where several farmers were driving their livestock on the way to slaughter, sheep and geese, ducks and even a few cows. There were wagons of goods there too, waiting to come into the city.

And beyond that, the horizon lay filled with woods. Woods that Kate longed to escape to.

Kate saw the carriage before Sophia did. It was pushing its way through the waiting vehicles, the occupants obviously assuming that they had the right to be first into the city proper. Maybe they did. The carriage was gilded and carved, with a family crest on the side that would probably have made sense if the nuns had thought such things worth teaching. The silk curtains were closed, but Kate saw one twitch open, revealing a woman within looking out from under an elaborate bird's-head mask.

Kate felt filled with envy and disgust. How could a few live so well?

"Look at them," Kate said. "They're probably on their way to a ball or a masquerade. They've probably never had to worry about being hungry in their lives."

"No, they haven't," Sophia agreed. But she sounded thoughtful, perhaps even admiring.

Then Kate realized what her sister was thinking. She turned to her, appalled.

"We can't just follow them," Kate said.

"Why not?" her sister shot back. "Why not try to get what we want?"

Kate didn't have an answer for her. She didn't want to tell Sophia that it wouldn't work. *Couldn't* work. That it wasn't the way the world fit together. They would take one look at them and *know* they were orphans, *know* they were peasants. How could they ever hope to blend into a world such as that?

Sophia was the elder sister; she was supposed to know all this already.

Besides, in that moment, Kate's eyes fell on something that was equally enticing to her. There were men forming up near the side of the square, wearing the colors of one of the mercenary companies that liked to dabble in the wars across the water. They had weapons laid out on carts, and horses. A few of them were even having an impromptu fencing tournament with blunted steel swords.

Kate eyed the weapons, and she saw what she needed: racks of steel. Daggers, swords, crossbows, traps for hunting. With even a few of these things, she could learn to trap and live off the land.

"Don't," Sophia said, watching her gaze, laying a hand on her arm.

Kate pulled free, but gently. "Come with me," Kate said, determined.

She saw her sister shake her head. "You know I can't. That isn't for me. It's not who I am. It's not what I want, Kate."

And trying to blend with a bunch of nobles wasn't what Kate wanted.

She could feel her sister's certainty, she could feel her own, and she had a sudden sense of where this was going. The knowledge of it made tears sting her eyes. She threw her arms around her sister, just as her sister embraced her.

"I don't want to leave you," Kate said.

"I don't want to leave you either," Sophia replied, "but maybe we need to each try our own way, at least for a little while. You are as stubborn as I, and we each have our own dream. I am convinced I can make it, and that then I can help you."

Kate smiled.

"And I am convinced *I* can make it, and then I can help you."

Kate could see the tears in her sister's eyes now too, but more than that, she could feel the sadness there through the connection they shared.

"You're right," Sophia said. "You wouldn't fit in at court, and *I* wouldn't fit in, in some wilderness, or learning to fight. So maybe we have to do this separately. Maybe our best chances of survival are by being apart. If nothing else, if one of us is caught, then the other can come rescue her."

Kate wanted to tell Sophia that she was wrong, but the truth was that everything she was saying made sense.

"I'll find you afterwards," Kate said. "I'll learn how to fight and how to live in the countryside, and I'll find you. Then you will see, and you will come join me."

"And I will find *you* when I've succeeded at court," Sophia countered with a smile. "You will join me in the palace and marry a prince, and rule over this town."

They each smiled wide, tears rolling down their cheeks.

But you won't ever be alone, Sophia added, the words ringing in Kate's mind. *I will always be as close as a thought.*

Kate couldn't bear the sadness anymore, and she knew she had to act before she changed her mind.

So she hugged her sister one last time, let go, and ran in the direction of the weapons.

It was time to risk it all.

CHAPTER FIVE

Sophia could feel the determination burning inside her as she set off across Ashton, making for the walled precinct where the palace lay. She hurried down the streets, dodging horses and occasionally hopping onto the back of wagons when it looked as though they might be heading in the right direction.

Even with that, it took time to cross the expanse of the place, moving through the Screws, the Merchant Quarter, Knotty Hill, and the other districts one by one. They were so strange and full of life after her time in the House of the Unclaimed that Sophia wished she had more time in which to explore them. She found herself standing outside a great circular theater, wishing that there were enough time to go inside.

There wasn't, though, because if she missed the masked ball tonight, she wasn't sure how she was going to find the place at court she wanted. A masked ball, even she knew, didn't come around very often, and it would offer her best chance to sneak in.

She worried about Kate as she went. It felt strange, after so long, simply walking in opposite directions. But the truth was that they wanted different things from their lives. Sophia would find her, when this was done. When she had a life settled among the nobles of Ashton, she would find Kate and make everything all right.

The gates to the walled precinct that held the palace lay ahead. As Sophia had expected, they were thrown open for the evening, and beyond them, she could see formal gardens laid out in neat rows of hedges and roses. There were even great expanses of grass, trimmed shorter than any farmer's field could be, and that in itself seemed like a sign of luxury when anyone else in the city who had a scrap of land beside their house had to use it to grow food.

There were lanterns set up on poles every few steps within the gardens. They weren't lit yet, but by night, they would turn the whole place into a wash of bright light, letting people dance on the lawns as easily as in one of the great rooms of the palace.

Sophia could see people heading inside, one after another. There was a gold-liveried servant by the gate, along with two guards in the brightest blue, their muskets shouldered in perfect parade ground display while nobles and their servants sauntered past.

Sophia hurried for the gate. She'd hoped that she could lose herself in a crowd of those coming in, but by the time she got there, she was the only one. It meant that the servant there was able to give her his full attention. He was an older man in a powdered wig that curled down to the nape of his neck. He looked at Sophia with something approaching disdain.

"And what do *you* want?" he demanded, in a tone so arch it might have been that of an actor playing at being noble, rather than the servant of the real thing.

"I'm here for the ball," Sophia said. She knew she could never pass for noble, but there were still things she could do. "I'm the servant of—"

"Don't embarrass yourself," the servant shot back. "I know perfectly well who is to be let in, and none of them would bother being accompanied by a servant like you. We're not letting in dock whores. It's not that kind of party."

"I don't know what you mean," Sophia tried, but the scowl she got back told her that it wasn't even close to working.

"Then allow me to explain," the servant on the door said. He seemed to be enjoying himself. "Your dress looks as though it has been cut down from a fishwife's. You stink as if you've just come out of a cess pit. As for your voice, you sound as though you couldn't even *spell* elocution, let alone employ it. Now, be off with you, before I have you run off and thrown in a lock-up for the night."

Sophia wanted to argue, but the cruelty of his words seemed to have stolen all of hers. More than that, they'd stolen away her dream, as easily as if the man had reached out and plucked it from the air. She turned and ran, and the worst part was the laughter that followed her all the way down the street.

Sophia stopped in a doorway further on, utterly humiliated. She hadn't expected this to be easy, but she'd expected someone in the city to be kind. She'd thought that she would be able to pass for a servant even if she couldn't pass for a noblewoman.

Maybe that was her mistake though. If she was trying to reinvent herself, shouldn't she go the whole way? Maybe it wasn't too late. She couldn't pass for the kind of servant who would accompany her mistress to a ball, but what could she pass for? She could be the thing she'd almost been when she left the orphanage. The kind of servant who would be given the lowest of jobs.

That might work.

The area around the palace was a place of noble townhouses, but also of all the things that their owners might want from the city:

dressmakers, jewelers, bathhouses, and more. All things that Sophia couldn't afford, but all things that she might be able to get anyway.

She started with a dressmaker. It was the biggest part of it, and maybe, once she had the dress, the rest would be easier. She walked into the shop that looked busiest, panting as if she were about to collapse, hoping for the best.

"What are you doing in here?" a steel-haired woman asked, looking up with a mouth full of pins.

"Forgive me…" Sophia said. "My mistress… she'll flog me if her dress is any later… she said… to run all the way."

She couldn't pass for a servant accompanying her mistress, but she could be that noble's indentured servant, sent on last-minute errands.

"And your mistress's name?" the dressmaker demanded.

Is this really the kind of servant that Milady D'Angelica might send? Perhaps it's because they're of a size and she wishes to know if it will fit?

The flicker of Sophia's talent came unbidden. She had more sense than to question it.

"Milady D'Angelica," she said. "Forgive me, but she said to hurry. The ball—"

"Will not start in earnest for another hour or two, and I doubt your mistress will want to be there until the moment to make an entrance," the dressmaker replied. Her tone was a little less harsh now, although Sophia suspected that was only because of who she was pretending to serve. The other woman pointed. "Wait there."

Sophia waited, although that was the hardest thing in the world to do right then. It gave her a chance to listen, at least. The servant at the palace had been right: people did speak differently away from the poorest parts of the city. Their vowels were more rounded, the edges of the words more polished. One of the women working there seemed to have come from one of the Merchant States, her accent making her r's roll as she chattered with the others.

It wasn't long before the original dressmaker came out with a dress, holding it up to Sophia for inspection. It was the single most beautiful thing Sophia had ever seen. It shone silver and blue, seeming to shimmer as it moved. The bodice was worked with silver thread, and even the underskirts shimmered in waves, which seemed like a waste. Who would see them?

"Milady D'Angelica and you are the same size, yes?" the dressmaker demanded.

"Yes, ma'am," Sophia replied. "It's why she sent me."

"Then she should have sent you in the first place, rather than just a list of measurements."

"I'll be sure to tell her," Sophia said.

That made the dressmaker pale with horror, as if the sheer thought of it were enough that it might give her a heart attack.

"There's no need for that. It's very close, but I just need to adjust a couple of things. You're *certain* that you are her size?"

Sophia nodded. "To the inch, ma'am. She has me eat exactly what she does so that we stay the same."

It was a wild, foolish detail to make up, but the dressmaker seemed to swallow it. Perhaps it was the kind of extravagance she believed a noblewoman might stoop to. Either way, she made the adjustments so fast that Sophia could barely believe it, finally handing her a package wrapped in patterned paper.

"The bill to go on Milady's account?" the dressmaker asked. There was a note of hope there, as if Sophia might have the money on her, but Sophia could only nod. "Of course, of course. I trust that Milady D'Angelica will be pleased."

"I'm sure she will be," Sophia said. She practically ran for the door.

Actually, she was sure that the noble would be furious, but Sophia didn't plan on being around for that part.

She had other places to go, for one thing, and other packages to "collect" on her "mistress's" behalf.

At a cobbler's shop, she collected boots of the finest pale leather, set off with etched lines showing a scene from the Nameless Goddess's life. At a perfumer's shop, she acquired a small vial that smelled as though its creator had somehow distilled the essence of everything beautiful into one fragrant combination.

"It is my greatest work!" he proclaimed. "I hope that Lady Beaufort enjoys it."

At each stop, Sophia picked a fresh noblewoman to be the servant of. That was simple practicality: she couldn't guarantee that Milady D'Angelica had been to every shop in town. With some of the shops, she picked the names from the owners' thoughts. With others, when her talent wouldn't come, she had to keep the conversation hovering until they made assumptions, or, in one case, until she could steal an upside-down glance at a log book over the shop's counter.

It seemed to get easier, the more she stole. Each preceding piece of her stolen outfit served as a kind of credential for the next, because obviously those other shopkeepers wouldn't have given things to the wrong person. By the time she arrived at the shop where they sold masks, the storekeeper was practically pressing his wares into her hands before she was through the doors. It was a half mask of carved ebony, scene after scene of the Masked Goddess seeking hospitality set off with feathers around the edges and pinpoints of jewels around the eyes. They were probably designed to make it seem as though the eyes of the wearer were shining with reflected light.

Sophia felt a small flash of guilt as she took it, adding it to the not inconsiderable pile of packages in her arms. She was stealing from so many people, taking things that they'd worked to produce, and that others had paid for. Or would pay for, or hadn't quite paid for; Sophia still hadn't wrapped her head around the ways in which nobles seemed to buy things without quite paying for them.

It was only a brief flash of guilt, though, because they all had so much compared to the orphans back in the House of the Unclaimed. Just the jewels on this mask would have changed their lives.

For now, Sophia needed to change herself, and she couldn't go into the party still filthy from sleeping beside the river. She walked around the bathhouses, waiting until she found one with carriages waiting by the door, and which advertised separate bathing for ladies of quality. She had no coins to pay, but she walked to the doors anyway, ignoring the look the large, muscular proprietor gave her.

"My mistress is within," she said. "She told me to fetch everything by the time she was finished bathing, or there would be trouble."

He looked her up and down. Again, the packages in Sophia's hands seemed to work like a passport. "Then you'd better get inside, hadn't you? The changing rooms are over on your left."

Sophia went to them, putting her stolen prizes down in a room that was hot with steam from the baths. Women came and went wearing the winding sheets that served to dry them. None of them looked twice at Sophia.

She undressed, wrapping a sheet around herself and heading into the baths. They were set out in the style they favored across the water, with multiple hot, warm, and cold pools, masseuses at the side, and waiting servants.

Sophia was all too aware of the tattoo on her ankle proclaiming what she was, but there were indentured servants there with their mistresses, there to massage them with scented oils or scrape combs through their hair. If anyone noticed the mark, they obviously assumed that Sophia was there for that reason.

Even so, she didn't take the time to luxuriate in the baths that she might have. She wanted to get out of there before anyone asked questions. She dunked herself under the water, scrubbing with soap and trying to get the worst of the dirt from her. When she stepped from the bath, she made sure that her winding sheet reached all the way to her ankles.

Back in the dressing room, she pieced her new self together one step at a time. She started with silk stockings and underskirts, then worked up through corsetry and outer skirts, gloves, and more.

"Does my lady require assistance with her hair?" a woman asked, and Sophia looked across to see a servant watching her.

"If you would," Sophia said, trying to remember how nobles talked. It occurred to her that this would be easier if no one thought she was from around there, so she added a hint of the Merchant States accent she'd heard at the dressmaker's. To her surprise, it came easily, her voice adjusting as quickly as the rest of her had.

The girl dried and braided her hair in an elaborate knot that Sophia could barely follow. When it was done, she settled her mask in place, then headed outside, making her way among the carriages there until she spotted one that wasn't taken.

"You there!" she called, her newfound voice seeming strange to her ears right then. "Yes, you! Take me to the palace at once, and don't stop along the way. I'm in a hurry. And don't start asking for the fare. You can send the bill to Lord Dunham and he can feel grateful that it's all I'm costing him tonight."

She didn't even know if there was a Lord Dunham, but the name felt right. She expected the carriage driver to argue, or at least dicker over the fare. Instead, he just bowed.

"Yes, my lady."

The carriage ride through the city was more comfortable than Sophia could have imagined. More comfortable than jumping on the back of wagons, certainly, and far shorter. In a matter of minutes, she could see the gates approaching. Sophia felt her heart tighten, because the same servant was still working on them. Could she do this? Would he recognize her?

The carriage slowed, and Sophia forced herself to lean out, hoping that she looked as she should.

"Is the ball in full swing yet?" she demanded in her new accent. "Have I arrived at the right time to make an impact? More to the point, how do I look? My servants tell me that this is suitable for your court, but I feel I look like some docksides whore."

She couldn't resist that small revenge. The servant on the gate bowed deeply.

"My lady could not have timed her arrival better," he assured her, with the kind of false sincerity that Sophia guessed nobles liked. "And she looks absolutely lovely, of course. Please, go straight through."

Sophia closed the curtain to the carriage as it drove on, but only so it would hide her stunned relief. This was working. It was actually working.

She just hoped that things were working out as well for Kate.

CHAPTER SIX

Kate was enjoying the city more than she would have thought possible alone. She still ached with the loss of her sister, and she still wanted to get out into the open countryside, but for now, Ashton was her playground.

She made her way through the city streets, and there was something particularly appealing about being lost in the crowds. Nobody looked her way, any more than they looked at the other urchins or apprentices, younger sons or would-be fighters of the town. In her boyish costume and with the short spikes of her hair, Kate could have passed for any of them.

There was so much to see in the city, and not just the horses that Kate cast a covetous eye over every time she passed one. She paused opposite a vendor selling hunting weapons out of a wagon, the light crossbows and occasional muskets looking impossibly grand. If Kate could have snatched one, she would have, but the man kept a careful eye on everyone who came close.

Not everyone was so careful, though. She managed to snatch a hunk of bread from a café table, a knife from where someone had used it to pin up a religious pamphlet. Her talent wasn't perfect, but knowing where people's thoughts and attention were was a big advantage when it came to the city.

She kept on, looking for an opportunity to take more of what she would need for life out in the country. It was spring, but that just meant rain instead of snow most days. What would she need? Kate started to check things off on her fingers. A bag, twine to make traps for animals, a crossbow if she could get one, an oilskin to keep the rain off, a horse. Definitely a horse, despite all the risks that horse thievery brought with it.

Not that any of it was truly safe. There were gibbets on some of the corners holding the bones of long dead criminals, preserved so that the lesson could last. Over one of the old gates, ruined in the last war, there were three skulls on spikes that were supposedly those of the traitor chancellor and his conspirators. Kate wondered how anybody knew anymore.

She spared a glance for the palace in the distance, but that was only because she hoped that Sophia was all right. That kind of place was for the likes of the dowager queen and her sons, the nobles and their servants trying to shut out the troubles of the real world with their parties and their hunts, not real people.

"Hey, boy, if you've got coin to spend, I'll show you a good time," a woman called from the doorway of a house whose purpose was obvious even if it had no sign. A man who could have wrestled bears stood on the door, while Kate could hear the sounds of people enjoying themselves too much even though it wasn't dark yet.

"I'm not a boy," she snapped back.

The woman shrugged. "I'm not picky. Or come in and make yourself some coin. The old lechers like the boyish ones."

Kate stalked on, not dignifying that with an answer. That wasn't the life she had planned for herself. Nor was stealing to gain everything she wanted.

There were other opportunities that seemed more interesting. Everywhere she looked, it seemed that there were recruiters for one or other of the free companies, declaring their high pay in relation to the others, or their better rations, or the glory to be won in the wars across the Knife-Water.

Kate actually wandered up to one of them, a hearty-looking man in his fifties, wearing a uniform that seemed better suited to a player's idea of war than the real thing.

"Ho there, boy! Are you looking for adventure? For derring-do? For the possibility of death at the swords of your enemies? Well, you've come to the wrong place!"

"The *wrong* place?" Kate said, not even caring that he too had thought she was a boy.

"Our general is Massimo Caval, the most famously cautious of fighting men. Never does he engage unless he can win. Never does he waste his men in fruitless confrontations. Never does he—"

"So you're saying he's a coward?" Kate asked.

"A coward is the best thing to be in a war, believe me," the recruiter said. "Six months running ahead of enemy forces while they get bored, with only occasional looting to liven things up. Think of it, the life, the… wait, you're not a boy, are you?"

"No, but I can still fight," Kate insisted.

The recruiter shook his head. "Not for us, you can't. Be off with you!"

In spite of his defense of cowardice, the recruiter looked as though he might cuff her around the head if Kate stayed there, so she kept walking.

So many things in the city made little sense. The House of the Unclaimed had been a cruel place, but at least it had possessed a kind of order. Half the time, in the city, it seemed that people did whatever they wanted, with little input from the city's rulers. The city itself certainly seemed to have no plan to it. Kate crossed a bridge that had been built up with stalls and stages and even small houses until there was barely enough room to use it for its intended purpose. She found herself walking down streets that spiraled back on themselves, down alleys that somehow became the roofs of houses at a lower elevation, then gave way to ladders.

As for the people on the streets, the whole city seemed insane. There seemed to be someone shouting on every corner, declaring the elements of their personal philosophy, demanding attention for the performance they were about to put on, or denouncing the kingdom's involvement in the wars across the water.

Kate ducked into doorways as she saw the masked figures of priests and nuns about the inscrutable business of the Masked Goddess, but after the third or fourth time she kept walking. She saw one flailing a chain of prisoners, and she found herself wondering what part of the goddess's mercy that represented.

There were horses everywhere in the city. They pulled carriages, they bore riders, and some of the larger ones pulled carts full of everything from stone to beer. Seeing them was one thing; stealing one was proving to be quite another.

In the end, Kate picked a spot outside an ostler's shop, moving closer and waiting for her moment. To steal something as big as a horse, she needed more than just a moment of inattention, but in principle it was no different from stealing a pie. She could feel the thoughts of the stable hands as they roved and wandered. One was bringing out a fine-looking mare, thinking about the noblewoman it was intended for.

Damn it, she'll need a side saddle, not this.

The thought was all the invitation Kate needed. She moved forward as the ostler rushed back inside, probably thinking that no one could take a horse in the brief space he would be gone. Kate wove her way in between the pedestrians who littered the street, imagining the moment when her hands would finally close around the reins—

"Got you!" a voice said as a hand clamped down on her shoulder.

For a moment, Kate thought that someone had guessed what she intended to do, but as the figure who'd grabbed her spun Kate back toward him, she recognized the truth: it was one of the boys from the orphanage.

She squirmed to get away, and he hit her, hard, catching her in the stomach. Kate fell down to her knees, and she saw two other boys coming up fast.

"They sent us out after you when you got away," the oldest of them said. "Said that girls went for more than boys, and that they could send hunters for all of us if necessary."

He sounded bitter about that, and Kate didn't blame him. The House of the Unclaimed was an evil place, but it was also the only home the orphans there had.

She *did* blame him for the next punch, which rocked her head back.

"That's for the beating you gave us with that poker of yours," he said. "And *this* is for the beating the priests gave us after."

He punctuated it with slaps that rocked Kate where she knelt.

"We've been out here more than a day now," the oldest said. "I'm hungry, I'm tired, and I want to go back. I'm due to go into the army soon, and you'll not ruin that for me. So I'm going to drag you back there, but not before you tell me where your bitch of a sister is."

Kate shook her head while he hit her again. She silently vowed vengeance for this moment, even though right then she couldn't even stand, let alone do anything about it all. She rolled up her hatred, tucking it deep inside with her anger at the sisters who'd brought her up so cruelly, and at the world that had stolen her parents in the first place.

Her hatred didn't do anything to keep the blows away, though, or deflect the questions that punctuated them like arrows.

"Where is your sister?" he demanded. "Where? She's the one they'll indenture for better coin."

"I don't know," Kate insisted. "I wouldn't tell you if I did."

She could see people walking past now. Some did it with fixed expressions, others glancing across then looking away as they decided that they didn't want to get involved. Kate saw a young man wearing the apron of a carpenter's apprentice walking past, and his thoughts flickered through her mind.

I wish I could help, but they're bigger than me, and maybe she deserves it, and what if—

"If you want to help, help!" Kate yelled across to him.

He turned in surprise, and actually started to step toward them out of sheer embarrassment.

"Stay out of this," the eldest of the boys snapped at him, but Kate didn't need more than just that single moment of distraction.

She kicked away from him like a swimmer pushing off from the shore, then scrambled to her feet and ran. Behind her, Kate heard the shouts of the boys following, but she ignored them and kept going, not even caring about the direction she took. She headed for the thickest parts of the crowd, thinking she could slip through while the others would be slowed, then took off down an alley at random, hoping to lose them.

It didn't work. Kate didn't have to look around to know that. She could feel their thoughts on her, honed to a sharp edge the way a hunting dog's might have been. The only promising sign was that one of Ashton's evening mists was coming down, making it harder to see anything, let alone one fleeing girl.

Kate ran down toward the river, on the basis that the mist was always thickest there when it came. Sure enough, it thickened into fog, so that Kate could barely see the length of the streets she ran down.

She reached a crumbling set of docks, against which plenty of small boats were mooring up for the night. Others were risking the fog, rowing through it or putting up small sails while guided by the light of oil-burning lamps.

Kate started to look around for somewhere to hide. She couldn't run from the boys chasing from her forever, but maybe she could wait until they'd passed by. Already, she couldn't see them in the fog; she could only hear them approaching. She headed out onto one of the crumbling piers used to moor the boats.

She'll hide on a boat. We need to search them.

That thought sent fear running through Kate. She'd been so certain that this would work, but now... she couldn't hide, she couldn't turn back. What *could* she do?

This way, a voice said in her mind, and this wasn't like reading the thoughts of the boys. It was more like the moments when her sister contacted her. *Jump to me.*

Kate turned and saw a barge going past, filled with the detritus of the city, lit by red and green lamps to show those approaching which way it was heading. A girl her age stood on the back, using a long wooden pole to guide it. As Kate watched, she lifted the pole from the water, holding it out.

Kate stood there in shock for a moment or two. She'd always thought that she and Sophia were unique; that they were alone in the world in that sense as well as all the others. The thought that there might be someone who could send her thoughts across to Kate was enough to make her freeze, trying to make sense of it.

What are you waiting for? Jump!

Kate flung herself forward, and even in springtime, the water was enough to knock the breath from her. They hadn't bothered teaching the girls to swim in the orphanage, so Kate spent a moment flailing before her hand closed around the pole the other girl was holding out.

She was stronger than she looked, reeling Kate in with the pole the way someone else might have hauled in a fish. Kate gasped as she pulled her way onto the barge.

"Here," the girl said, holding out a blanket. "You look like you need it."

Kate took it, gratefully. While she wrapped it around herself, she looked at the other girl, who was small, blonde, and streaked with the dirt of the things she shepherded down the river. She wore a leather apron over a dress that had probably been blue once, although now it was closer to brown.

"I'm Kate," she managed.

The other girl smiled. "Emeline. Quiet now. Whoever's after you, they won't see us in the mist."

Kate huddled down in the stern of the boat, watching the docks, or at least what she could see of them. They were quickly fading away behind a wall of fog as the barge kept moving.

As they disappeared from view completely, Kate dared to breathe a sigh of relief. She'd done it.

She'd escaped them.

CHAPTER SEVEN

Sophia could hardly believe that she was inside the palace. Back at the House of the Unclaimed, it had seemed like a magical place; another world that the likes of her could only hope to set foot in if they found themselves indentured to the right nobles through some special skill.

Now, she was there, thanks to little more than the willingness to fool those who wanted to believe in her, and the courage to actually try. Sophia couldn't help a note of amazement at that, and at the space around her.

It was beautiful, it was elegant, and it was about as far from the orphanage as any building could hope to be. Instead of cramped conditions, there were high ceilings and spacious rooms that seemed to have been designed more as displays of opulence than simply as places to live. There were soft chairs and chaises carved in the elaborate style that had come in from across the water, thick carpets from the water looms of the Merchant States, and even a few worked silver statuettes from further off, in the lands where it was said that men had never even heard of the Masked Goddess.

This palace was everything Sophia had ever wanted.

No, not everything. This was a beautiful place to be, but it wasn't enough to simply get here. Sophia had to find a way to stay. She'd come here in the hopes that there would be a way to find a life among the nobles. A way to be safe.

Sophia didn't feel very safe right then. There were paintings on the walls of beautiful women and strong-looking men, probably representing different facets of the kingdom's noble lines. Right then, Sophia probably looked like one of the women, but she felt as though that façade was as thin as one of the canvases, easy to tear through and likely to fall away at any moment.

"Focus," she told herself, trying to act the way she thought a foreign noblewoman would on arriving in the palace. She walked through the crowds of people there, smiling beneath her half mask and nodding, pausing to admire paintings and sculptures.

There were nobles there—other nobles, Sophia corrected herself—standing in groups and laughing amongst themselves as they waited for the ball to begin. She saw a group of young women of perhaps her age, all wearing dresses that had probably taken

38

someone weeks of work to produce. One, resplendent in a gossamer blue gown that seemed designed to show off her figure, was complaining to the others from beneath the ivory oval of her mask.

"I sent my servant there, and you'll never guess what happened. Someone had *taken* my dress. *My* dress!"

Sophia held her breath, feeling certain that at any moment, the girl would turn and see her; would spot the dress she was wearing and denounce her as not just a fraud but a thief. Sophia guessed that this was "Milady D'Angelica," as the dressmaker had called her.

"I never even got to see my dress," the girl continued, and Sophia dared to breathe a sigh of relief. "I had to settle for one the dressmaker had ready for some burgher's daughter."

One of the others, whose mask formed an elaborate bird's beak, laughed. "At least that means there will be less riffraff in here."

The others laughed along with her, and the girl who had been complaining about her dress nodded.

"Come on," she said. "It will be time for the dancing soon, and I want my makeup just so, if some handsome young man happens to unmask me. Perhaps one of the dowager's sons will want to kiss me."

"Angelica, you *are* daring," one of the others said.

Sophia hadn't thought of that. She'd come here with some half-formed thought of being able to fit in at court and marry some rich man, but she hadn't thought enough to consider what she would do if she had to take her mask off. Presumably, somewhere in between her coming to the party and living happily ever after, someone would want to see her face?

So she followed them, trying not to make it look too obvious as she went, pausing to look at the statuary there.

"Ah, you're admiring the latest Hollenbroek," a fat man said.

A truly awful thing, but it's what I'm expected to say.

"I think it's awful," Sophia said, with the slight fleck of an accent she'd picked out to let the nobles forgive any of her mistakes. "Excuse me, though, I still need to do my makeup for the ball."

"Then perhaps we can dance later," he suggested. "If you have your dance card…"

"My dance card?" Sophia asked, puzzled. She couldn't see the man frown beneath his mask, but she could feel his confusion. "Yes, of course. I don't seem to have it with me at the moment."

She walked away swiftly even though she knew it was rude. It was better than being found out because she didn't know the rules that these people had. Besides, the noble girls were almost out of sight.

Sophia followed them to a small antechamber, glancing inside to see a girl perhaps a couple of years older than she wearing the gray of an indentured servant, standing there surrounded by mirrors and brushes while the girls sat themselves on high-backed chairs in front of her. The servant had dark hair that fell short of her shoulders, and features that might have been pretty if she'd been allowed to use any of the tools of her trade on herself. As it was, she mostly looked overworked.

"Well then," the first noble girl snapped. "What are you waiting for?"

"If my lady would care to remove her mask?" the girl suggested.

The noblewoman did it with bad grace, muttering something about rude servants, while the others did the same. They set their masks beside them, like upturned faces, but Sophia was more interested in watching their real features. Some of them were good-looking, some plainer featured but still with the smooth skin that came from expensive lotions and the confidence that came from knowing they could buy half the city if they wanted. Probably only Milady D'Angelica was truly beautiful, though, with features that could have come from one of the paintings adorning the walls, and an air of sharp superiority that said she knew exactly how beautiful she was.

"Get on with it," she said. "And be careful. I've had a very trying day today."

Presumably not as trying as that of a servant having to wait on her, or as someone risking her freedom trying to sneak into the festivities. Still, Sophia didn't say anything. Instead, she watched as the serving girl started work with powders and paints, subtly transforming the features of each of the nobles she worked on.

"Work faster!" one of them snapped. "Honestly, these indentured girls are so *lazy*."

"That's not all they are," another replied. "Did you hear that Henine Watsworth caught one in bed with her fiancé? No morals, any of them."

"And the way they look," Angelica added. "You can see the coarseness of their features. I don't know why we bother to mark them as what they are. You can spot it a mile away anyway."

They didn't seem to care that the servant was standing right there, or that she couldn't talk back because of her position. Sophia hated that cruelty. In fact—

40

"Excuse me, my lady," a passing servant asked. "But are you lost?"

It took Sophia a moment to remember that they might mean her. "No, no, I'm fine."

"Then would you care to go in for your makeup? I'm sure that another chair could be found."

The last thing Sophia wanted was to have to sit in there with the others, unmasked, where she was sure that someone would guess what she was. Or, more precisely, what she wasn't.

Sophia heard a snippet of the woman's thoughts, and it didn't do anything to reassure her.

Is she all right? I don't recognize her. Maybe I should—

"Do you think I need such things?" Sophia demanded in her haughtiest voice. "More to the point, do you think I want to be trapped in there with such chatter? Already, I can feel one of my headaches beginning. Go and fetch me water, girl. Go."

It felt as though she was playing a role in moments like that, the sharpness of it serving like the spikes of a thorn bush to keep people from getting too close. The servant hurried off, and so did Sophia. She couldn't stand out in the open like that.

Instead, she found a nook where she could hide, pretending to look at the paintings there, listening all the while for the moment when the room beyond would be empty. Sophia didn't even want to risk the servant seeing her. As the nobles had said, it was too easy to spot one of the indentured.

So she listened with her ears, and with her mind, waiting for the moment when it was quiet, then slipped back into the room with all the caution of a thief. Sophia seated herself in front of the mirrors there, removing her mask and considering the vast array of pigments and powders there.

She realized in that moment that she had no real idea of what to do. She knew what makeup was, she'd even seen a few women wearing it, but it had not been something allowed in the orphanage. The masked sisters would probably have beaten her even for asking about it. Why decorate the face when their goddess had hidden hers from the world? To them, only whores wore such things.

Even so, Sophia tried. She focused on what she thought the women in the paintings had looked like, and grabbed for the most likely-looking powders. It took her less than a minute to realize her mistake, as she went from looking like herself to some kind of demented clown, fit only for the least subtle of street theater.

"Hello?"

Sophia spun at the sound of the servant's voice, realized what she must look like, and grabbed for her mask. To her surprise, the servant was faster, catching her hand and gently pulling it away.

"No, no, don't do that. It will make things worse. Let me see, my lady…"

Who is she? I'm sure I know her.

"It will be fine," Sophia said, standing. It was only as she did so that she realized that she'd let her faint trace of an accent slip. She'd fallen back into her normal voice, and even she could hear how rough and uncultured that sounded compared to the nobles.

"Who are you?" the servant asked. She moved to look at Sophia. "Wait, I know you, don't I?"

"No, no, you're mistaken," Sophia managed. She should have pulled away then. She should have knocked the servant over and run. She didn't, though.

"Yes I do," the girl said. "You're Sophia. I remember you and your sister from the House of the Unclaimed. I'm Cora. I was only a couple of years older than you both, remember?"

Sophia started to shake her head, but the truth was that she did remember the other girl, and at that point, it seemed that there was no point in denying it.

"Yes," she said. "Yes, I remember."

"But what are you doing *here*?" Cora asked. "Come on, sit down. There must be a story in all of this."

Sophia had expected her to call for guards there and then, so she sat down almost as much from surprise as anything else. While she sat there, Cora started to wipe away the makeup from her face with expert hands.

Sophia told her what had happened. She told her about running away with her sister, and about sleeping rough in the city. She told her about parting from Kate to try to find happiness and safety in the ways that seemed to make most sense to them.

"And you're here because you think you can walk in and find a place at court?" Cora asked. Sophia waited for the other girl to tell her how stupid it was. "It *might* work, I suppose, if you were able to get the right people to become your friends, or more than friends. If you could persuade some nobleman to take you as his mistress… or his wife."

She laughed at that, as though it were preposterous, but for Sophia, that was the one option that seemed to make the most sense. It was the one option that left her safe. The truth was, though, that she would do what she had to do. She would become some noble's hanger-on, or friend, or courtesan, if that was what it took.

42

"So you don't think it's stupid?" Sophia asked. "You don't think it's an evil thing to try to do?"

"Evil?" Cora countered. "Evil is the fact that they can take us and sell us like chattel, with no real chance to ever repay the debts they say we owe. Evil is the part where noble girls get to treat me like nothing, even though all they do is stand around, waiting for the right husband. You do what you have to do to survive, Sophia. So long as it doesn't actually hurt someone else, do it and don't think twice. I wish I'd had the bravery to do what you're doing."

Sophia didn't feel very brave right then. "You didn't answer me about it being stupid. I mean, if one person guesses and hands me in—"

"It won't be me," Cora promised her. "And yes, it could be stupid, but only if you do it badly. The fact that you're here says you've been thinking about some of it, but have you thought it through? Who are you meant to be?"

"I thought I'd be a girl from the Merchant States," Sophia said, falling into the trace of an accent she'd chosen. "Here…"

The truth was that she hadn't thought of a reason.

"Being from across the water is good," Cora said. "Even the accent is close enough to fool most people. Say that you're here because of the wars. Your father was a minor noble from Meinhalt; it's a town from in the old League. I've heard people talking about the battles there wiping it out, so no one will be able to check. It will also explain why you don't have anything with you."

Sophia of Meinhalt. It sounded good.

"Thank you," Sophia said. "I would never—how do you know all this?"

Cora smiled. "People forget I'm there while I'm working on them. They talk, and I listen. Talking of which, sit there, and I'll… well, not make you beautiful, you're beautiful already, but make you what they expect."

Sophia sat, and the other girl started to work, picking out foundation and rouge, eye shadow and lip color.

"How much do you know about the etiquette here?" Cora asked. "Do you know who people are?"

"I don't know enough," Sophia admitted. "Before, a fat man asked me for my dance card, and I don't even know what that is. He started talking about someone called Hollenbroek, and I *think* I did the right thing, but I'm not sure."

"Hollenbroek is an artist," Cora explained. "Your dance card is a scrap of bone or ivory or slate to write the names of promised

43

dance partners on. And if there's a fat man asking about both, the odds are it's Percy d'Auge. Avoid him, he's a penniless lecher."

She went on about the others there, the nobles and their families, the dowager and her two sons, Prince Rupert and Prince Sebastian.

"Prince Rupert stands to inherit," she said. "He's... well, everything you expect a prince to be: dashing, handsome, arrogant, useless. Sebastian is different, they say. He's quieter. But you don't need to worry about them. You need some minor nobleman, Phillipe van Anter, perhaps."

As Cora went on, it became increasingly obvious to Sophia that she could never remember all of it. When she said as much, Cora shook her head.

"Don't worry. Being from across the water, no one will expect you to know all of it. In fact, it would be suspicious if you did. There, I think you're almost ready."

Sophia looked at herself in the mirror. It was her, and yet somehow also not her. It was certainly a more beautiful version of her than anything she could have imagined. It was impossibly far from what she'd have been able to do for herself.

"One more thing," Cora said. "I like the boots, but we both know what lies underneath. Take them off, and I'll disguise your mark. No one will know."

Sophia took her boots and stockings off, revealing the mark on her calf. Cora rubbed thick foundation over the spot, blending it in until it disappeared completely.

"There," she said. "Now, if you seduce some minor nobleman, you won't have to keep your boots on in bed."

"Thank you," Sophia said, hugging her. "Thank you so much for doing this."

Cora smiled. "I'm lucky. I have a job I'm actually good at, in a place I don't mind too much. But if I can help another like me, I will. And who knows? Maybe, once you're a wealthy noblewoman, you'll need a maid who knows how to make you look your best."

Sophia nodded; she wouldn't forget this. She stood in front of the mirrors, feeling now as if she were some old-fashioned knight, armored for battle. When she put on her mask, it was like pulling down her visor.

She was ready for battle.

CHAPTER EIGHT

Kate's dreams were of the orphanage, which meant that they were of violence. She was standing in a classroom. Figures surrounded her, dressed in the robes of the nuns or in the plain tunics of the boys there.

They asked her questions that made no sense, about stupid things: the proper way to embroider a pillow, the principal exports of Southern Issettia. Things Kate couldn't hope to answer.

They hit her with every failure. The sisters lashed out with belts or canes, while the boys simply used their fists. All the time, they chanted the same thing.

"You're not fit to be a free girl. You're not fit to be a free girl."

Kate felt hands on her and she tried to twist and fight back. She turned to scratch and punch and bite, and it was only as she came back to herself that she realized that the hands holding her weren't those of the boys or the Masked Sisters. Instead, Emeline stood over her, with a finger to her lips.

"Quiet," she said. "Too much noise, and you'll wake the barge hands."

Kate managed to get a grip on herself in time to keep from shouting out of sheer contrariness and panic.

"I thought you were the barge hand," Kate managed.

She saw Emeline shake her head. "They're sleeping up front. Said they'd carry me upriver if I guided the boat while they slept."

Kate didn't feel quite as safe then. Her new friend had saved her, and Kate had assumed that it was just the two of them on the boat, making their way down the wide river. Now, there were men she didn't know there somewhere, and a part of Kate wanted to go up to them and shove them off the boat just for the crime of daring to be there.

She didn't really. It was just that she needed to hit *something* then, and the orphanage's inhabitants weren't close at hand. She wanted to go back there and burn it to the ground, just so that she could be sure that it was gone from her life. She wanted revenge for every humiliation and blow that had been landed on her in the years she'd been there.

"Hey, you're safe now," Emeline said. "There's no need to worry. The ones who were chasing you won't catch you now."

Kate nodded, but there was a part of her that still didn't believe it. The House of the Unclaimed wasn't a place you left behind. Instead, it was somewhere to carry with you, always there no matter how far you ran. Maybe it was one reason why they didn't bother to lock the doors.

In an effort to ignore it all, Kate looked around at the city. In the evening light, the fog that had encompassed it was starting to burn away, revealing the wide expanse of the river stretching out on either side of them, lit by sailors' lamps and cut through with small sandbanks and eddy currents, patches of faster water and slow, meandering stretches.

The city on either side seemed just as varied. There were wooden buildings mixed with stone ones, some standing in orderly rows, others reaching out like fingers into the space belonging to the flowing water. Some of the buildings obviously used the river for their business, with pulley systems or jetties showing the spots where goods were loaded and unloaded. Others were simply there with views out over the water for wealthy inhabitants.

Kate saw one man sitting there, trying to paint the river scene by lamplight, and she found herself wondering why anyone would bother. It wasn't beautiful, out there, was it? The city impinged on it too much for that. The water had the earthy sediment-and-sewage-filled smell of a waterway that people just threw things into. The river's surface was too full of boats and barges to see the reeds along the edges, or the birds that flitted amongst them. It wasn't anywhere that she would have wanted to paint.

"Careful," Emeline said as Kate started to stand up. "There are bridges ahead. You don't want to hit your head."

Kate dutifully sat back down again, looking ahead to where there was indeed a long bridge stretching across the river, low enough that probably only low barges like this one could get past it.

"They have to have separate docks on the other side," Emeline said. "Only the barges can go through without hitting their masts on it."

She pushed with her long steering pole as they got closer, lining the barge up with one of the bridge's arches. Kate could see spikes there, with the heads of criminals preserved in pitch so that they wouldn't rot as quickly. She wondered what their crimes were. Theft? Treason? Something in between?

There were open spaces by the side of the river as well as buildings. In those spaces, Kate saw men drilling for war, working with wooden muskets and crossbows because no one wanted to spend money on the real thing for mere recruits. Some of them were drilling in squares with pikes, while a few, probably officers, were fencing in front of the others with rapiers.

"You look as though you want to swim across and join them," Emeline said.

"Wouldn't you?" Kate said. "To be that strong, with no one to tell you what to do again."

Emeline laughed at that. "In one of the mercenary crews? All they *have* is people giving them orders. Besides, would you want to go across the Knife-Water and risk your life for some cause that doesn't mean anything?"

Kate wasn't sure about that. Put the way Emeline said it, the idea sounded like folly, but it also sounded like a chance of adventure.

"Besides, you might not have to go abroad if the rumors are true," Emeline said.

With most people, Kate would have read their thoughts to try to understand what they meant, but when she reached out for the other girl's, she couldn't see inside.

Kate, Emeline sent, *don't you know that's rude?*

"I'm sorry," Kate said. She didn't want to upset her new friend. "What did you mean, though?"

"Just that wars have a habit of not staying where you want them," Emeline replied. "People talk as though the Knife-Water is some unassailable gap, rather than just twenty miles of calm sea."

Kate hadn't thought about it that way. When she'd heard about the wars across the water between the fragmented states there, it had always seemed like something happening on the other side of the world. In truth, parts of the lands there were probably closer to Ashton than the watermills of the north, or the granite mountain spaces beyond that.

"So, you're not planning to run off and join one of the companies," Kate said. "What then? Why are you finding rides to take you upriver?"

Emeline half closed her eyes, and Kate knew that there was some daydream or other flickering behind those eyelids.

"For Stonehome," Emeline said in a voice that seemed caught up in the rapture of it for a moment.

"Stonehome?" Kate said. "What's that?"

She saw the other girl's eyes widen in surprise. "You don't know? But you… you're like me. You can hear thoughts!"

She probably said that a little louder than she intended. Certainly, it was the loudest thing she'd said since Kate had woken up.

"Stonehome is a place for people like us," Emeline said. "They say that it's a place where we can be safe, and others won't attack us for what we can do."

Kate wasn't sure that she believed such a place could exist. She barely believed that other people with the same gift as her were out there in the world. She'd been so sure that it was just her and her sister, for so long.

"You're sure this place exists?" Kate asked. It barely seemed possible.

"I've... heard rumors," Emeline said. "I'm not sure where it is exactly. If it were in the open, it would be too dangerous. They say it's out past the Ridings somewhere. I figured that I could focus on getting out of the city, then find it afterwards. I mean, people go there; it can't be impossible to find."

It seemed to be a lot for the other girl to pin her hopes on, but at least the boat was a good way for them to get out of the city. And maybe trying to find a place where those like them could be safe wasn't such a bad dream to have.

"What was it like, in the orphanage?" Emeline asked.

Kate shook her head. "Worse than you could imagine. They treated us as if we weren't even people, not really. Just inconvenient things to be shaped and sold."

It was what they'd been, in a way. The House of the Unclaimed pretended to be a place of safety for abandoned children, but in fact, it was a kind of factory for indentured servants, existing to provide them with skills that would make them useful once they reached an age to be sold.

"What about you?" Kate asked. "How did you come to be on a boat like this?"

Emeline shrugged. "I lived out on the streets for a while. It was... hard."

Kate knew how much pain could fit into a pause like that one. She reached out to wrap an arm around the other girl.

"I used to keep watch for... well, they were thieves, basically," Emeline said. "They'd go into eating houses and inns, and they'd walk out in other people's clothes, complete with whatever was in the pockets. I could tell them when there were people paying attention to them."

Kate thought of the ways she'd had to use her own powers to steal. "What happened?"

Emeline shrugged. "I caught some of their thoughts. They were thinking of getting rid of me. They thought I was too soft-hearted."

Kate could guess how hard that must have been. She was about to offer her new friend sympathy when she heard the sound of footsteps. *This* was what she hated about her talent: that it was so hit and miss. Why couldn't it warn her about every potential problem?

She turned in time to see a large barge hand standing over them, his barrel chest straining at the limits of his beer-stained shirt, hands closing into fists.

"A witch child! I let a witch child onto my barge? And there are two of you now? No, I won't have it! Get off my barge."

"Wait a minute," Kate said.

"Get off my barge, I said," he snapped. He snatched Emeline's steering pole from her easily, holding it the way one of the soldiers on the banks might have held a pike. "They say witches can't swim. Let's find out!"

He struck at Emeline first, knocking her back into the water as she gave a small sound of surprise. Kate stood, squaring up to the man, wishing then that she had a sword with which to stab him.

She didn't, though, and there was nowhere on the barge to dodge as the pole came swinging around in an arc. She felt the air rush out of her with the impact of it as it struck her in the abdomen, and for a moment, Kate felt herself airborne.

The water of the river hit her in a cold slap across her entire body. Kate sank, and for a moment she found herself wondering if maybe the barge hand had been right about her not floating. Then she kicked, bobbing to the surface like a cork and gasping for breath.

It didn't last for long. There was another boat coming straight toward her. Kate managed to push away from it in time, but the movement sent her back under the water again. She found herself looking up at the hulls of the passing boats, trying to find a clear space to come up in.

The water was cold, even in the heat of the day. Cold enough that Kate's body wanted to gasp with it, but she resisted the urge. She swam for the surface, managing to come up between two boats sculling themselves along with large oars.

"Help me!" Kate called out, but the men on them laughed.

"You'll have to swim for it, whelp," one called back. "No place for your sort here."

Kate wished that she could stab them all right then, but she could barely even keep her head above the water. She looked around, trying to find Emeline, but there was no sign of her there.

Had she been pulled away by the currents of the river, or… no, she wouldn't think like that.

Emeline? Kate sent, or tried to. Her powers weren't consistent at the best of times, and drowning in the middle of a river was not the best of times. She thought she caught a glimpse of a bobbing head somewhere between more boats, and tried to swim in that direction.

The currents wouldn't let her. What had seemed like gentle eddies when she'd been on the boat now turned out to be stronger things that snatched at Kate's limbs and threatened to pull her under at any moment. There was no way she could swim in the direction Emeline had been. It was all she could do to swim sideways, across the current, aiming for the bank while the river swept her downstream.

She tried to get a grip on the bridge as the river pulled her back through it, but the brickwork was too slick with moss and slime. She kept swimming on the far side, hoping that if she could just get to one of the banks, she could run along, spot Emeline, and maybe throw her a rope or something. Help her, somehow.

This side of the bridge was, if anything, even busier. There were oars cutting through the water, and poles, and keels, so that Kate had to dodge with every stroke she swam. Finally, *finally*, she found herself in calmer water, and her aching muscles managed to pull her closer to the far bank. Kate felt her hands close over a jetty, and she succeeded in pulling herself up.

For a minute or more, she lay there on the wood of the thing, sucking in air. Her arms burned from fighting the current. Her clothes were soaked and filthy from immersion in the cold water of the river. She felt, right then, as though she might just curl up and die there.

Instead, Kate sat up, forcing herself to scan the river for signs of Emeline.

Are you there? she sent, hoping for some reply from the other girl, but her powers were never as simple as that. Kate had only just learned that she could communicate with someone other than her sister; the odds of being able to connect to Emeline again seemed remote. The best that Kate could hope for was to spot the other girl floating down the river, borne there by the currents.

Yet she'd gone into the water first. She might already have been swept further downstream. Kate tried to run along the bank looking for her, but she didn't have the strength for it, and in any case, it was hopeless. She saw no sign of the other girl. At best, she had been swept ashore miles away. At worst, she would be dead somewhere under the water.

That thought made Kate's stomach knot, but the truth was that there was nothing she could do.

She stopped and looked around. She didn't know where she was in Ashton now. She'd been trying to get out of the city, but the river had carried her back a long way. She was alone again, wet, tired, cold, and alone.

Kate knelt down and cried.

Sophia, she sent. *Where are you?*

She waited, too long, in the silence, until she finally realized her sister could not hear her.

CHAPTER NINE

Sophia made her way back through the palace, trying to look more confident than she felt. From what she'd seen of the noble girls around there so far, they never admitted to a single moment of uncertainty.

It helped that she could see the crowds starting to form, drifting through the castle with a cluster of others. She caught some of the looks they gave her, and for a moment or two, she was worried they saw through her disguise. When one of the older women came up to her, Sophia was sure that they would unmask her, and send her back to the orphanage. Her talent gave her some reassurance.

Who is she? Must be new. We'd all have noticed a girl that beautiful, I'm sure. Reminds me a little of myself at that age. I'm sure there will be rumors.

"Welcome," the older woman said, offering her hand. "I am Lady Olive Casterston."

"Sophia... of Meinhalt," Sophia said, taking the woman's hand, remembering both her adopted voice and name just in time. "I'm very pleased to meet you."

Oh, from the Merchant States. No wonder I haven't heard of her. I suppose it explains the way she took my hand with no curtsey, too.

Sophia stretched her talents out as she talked, reading what she could from the woman. She didn't seem suspicious. If anything, she seemed determined to be friendly. They chattered about nothing, and Sophia used it as a moment to keep reading the room.

"Forgive me if my habits are not what you are used to," Sophia said. "Things are... very different here, I think."

"I hope not too different," Lady Olive said. "But I suppose, with the war... oh, you poor thing. Were you caught up in all that? Come on, come with me. I'll introduce you to people. Sir Jeffrey, this is Sophia of Meinhalt, you simply *must* meet her."

Just like that, Sophia found herself meeting a string of people so quickly that it was impossible to keep track of who was who. Lady Olive stayed with her for the first few, presenting a picture of a girl fleeing from the wars on the continent that meant Sophia never had to tell an outright lie, just... let people go on thinking what they were thinking.

52

She *knew* what they were thinking, of course, and her powers were the only reason she kept afloat in the sea of people she had to meet. They let her get glimpses of what these people expected, and catch fragments of information that let them think she had at least *heard* about the politics of Ashton.

She let the tide of people she simply had to meet carry her to the ballroom, and there, Sophia had to fight back the urge to gasp at the sheer spectacle of it all.

"Is everything all right, dear?" a retired officer asked her, clearly hoping for a chance to be gallant. Obviously, she hadn't done such a good job of disguising her shock at it all.

How could she, though? Every wall of the ballroom was mirrored, the mirrors surrounded by golden frames. The floor was a masterpiece of inlaid wood, forming a map of the known world that even contained some of the discovered lands beyond the ocean. There were chandeliers above that looked as though they held a thousand candles between them, while a trio of gold-clad musicians occupied a small space to one side. There was no space on the walls for paintings, but the architects had made up for it with a fresco above them in the modern style, making it look as though the ballroom opened out onto some great pastoral landscape.

"Miss?"

"Yes, I'm fine," Sophia assured him. "It's just that I never thought I would see an occasion like this... again." Sophia of Meinhalt would have attended such things before, of course. "Thank you for asking, though."

There was no dancing yet. Instead, those attending ate quails' eggs and wine-poached apples, drank delicate wines from goblets or took them over to what appeared to be a small fountain in one corner, flowing with the deep red of it.

Mostly, though, they appeared to jockey for position like folk at a market looking for the best bargains, or like armies seeking the highest ground. Perhaps both, because there certainly seemed to be a little of each thing in the room. The fragments of thought Sophia grasped made it clear that there was more than just dancing going on.

Surely I can't rank below him?

How did the Earl of Charlke afford the new house he's talking about?

Will my daughter find a husband tonight? She's nearly twenty*!*

Sophia had held an image of things like this as stately, graceful affairs, but the flickering thoughts of those around her made it clear just how much was going on beneath the surface. It seemed as though every gesture, every word, was a part of some greater game of position and advancement. Everyone there seemed to be attending because they wanted something, even if it was just to show the power and position they already possessed.

There *was* grace there, though. Some of the girls there looked as elegant as swans in their costumes, while everyone seemed to have done their best with their outfits and their masks. It was the kind of occasion that somewhere else might have made everyone anonymous, but here served more to show off their taste and their ability to afford the finest things.

Or steal them, in Sophia's case.

She glided through the room with delicate steps, listening to both the gossip that the nobles traded among themselves and the deeper layer beneath it that they only thought. She heard rumors about which men and women had lost at cards or betting on horses, alongside deeper worries from those who suspected that this time they might not be able to pay their debts. She heard the stories of affairs and infidelities, and her talent let her pick out the ones that were true from the ones that were being spread deliberately to cause trouble.

Perhaps if she'd been a different kind of person, Sophia might have tried to make her fortune by dealing in those secrets. That wasn't what she wanted, though. She wanted to be happy, not hated. She wanted to be a part of this place, not a predator on its edges. She wanted to be more than just the gift that she had.

That meant finding a more permanent way to connect to this court. It meant finding a husband here. Sophia swallowed at the thought of that. It was a big commitment to make, and put like that, it sounded incredibly mercenary. Yet, was it any worse than the nobles standing around trying to make good marriages with one another, or for their offspring?

It was definitely better than being indentured, whatever happened.

And, in one way, Sophia had an advantage over the others there: she could at least see what kind of people the men around her really were. She could look deep into them and see that the upright man to her left had a streak of cruelty to him, or spot the young man thinking about the courtesan he would visit again tonight.

Sophia looked around the room, felt the eyes on her, felt the hopes of some of the men who glanced her way. Some of them felt predatory, like wolves circling a deer. Some clearly wanted to use her and discard her.

There was one young man wearing a sun mask and cloth of gold costume that only served to emphasize the handsome lines of his features. He stood at the center of a clutch of hangers-on, and Sophia knew even before she glanced through their thoughts that this was Rupert, the dowager's eldest son and heir to the realm.

A glance at *his* thoughts made Sophia look away. To him, she was nothing more than a piece of meat. Worse, beneath that joking façade, there was a touch of violence. Sophia had heard that Prince Rupert was a fine soldier who liked to train alongside the other noble officers. There was more than that, though, and it was enough to make Sophia certain that she didn't want to go near him.

She started to concentrate on looking for the nobleman Cora had recommended: Phillipe van Anter. But trying to pick one specific person out of a masked crowd was difficult, even with a talent such as hers. She looked at a tall young man with hair as red as hers. No, it wasn't him. Nor was it a man dressed in a harlequin costume or one who thought that his military uniform made a perfectly good costume.

She turned and froze in place as she saw a young man on the edge of the crowds there. He was richly dressed, in a costume that seemed to evoke the flowing water and shifting weather of the island kingdom. He wore a gray and silver tunic over a blue shirt and hose, with lightly jeweled boots that somehow managed to be elegant rather than overstated.

The mask hid half his face, but even with it, Sophia could see that he was handsome. He didn't have the hard edges of some of the soldiers in the room, but he still seemed strong and athletic.

He wasn't one of those leering at her, or at the other young women in the room. Sophia caught none of the sense of violence from him that she'd gotten from Prince Rupert, and none of the problems that she'd seen in so many other thoughts there. There was something quiet about him, almost peaceful.

That wasn't how Sophia felt, though. She could feel herself breathing faster at the sight of him, and her eyes stayed locked to him as he moved around the room. It was only as a man bowed low in front of him that she picked up the one thing she hadn't realized:

This was Prince Sebastian, younger son of the dowager. Not the one who would ever inherit, but still far more than she could ever hope for.

Sophia started to look away, but found her gaze drawn back to him as if she couldn't stop it. On the way there, she caught sight of Lady D'Angelica and her friends, and even if she hadn't been able to read her thoughts, Sophia would have seen the hungry look the noblewoman gave the prince.

When she did look at Angelica's thoughts, Sophia froze.

One drink, and he'll soon be sleepy enough.

Sophia made her way toward the other girl through the chattering crowd. Sophia saw her touch a pouch set at her waist.

I just hope that the physiker didn't cheat me. If this doesn't work fast enough, I'll never be the one to get him to his bed.

Sophia could guess at her plan now. Angelica was planning to give Prince Sebastian some kind of sedative, then go out of the hall on his arm. She was going to trick him into bed with her, regardless of his wishes.

When I'm with child, he'll have to marry me.

That intercepted thought pushed Sophia over the edge. She had to stop this. She snuck up close behind the other girl, using her talent the way she'd used it to steal on the street, watching for the moment Angelica's attention wandered, and then reaching out as calmly as waving a fan to snatch the bag from her belt.

Sophia could have thrown the sedative away, but right then, she felt that the noblewoman deserved more than that—for what she'd been like with Cora, if nothing else. Sophia took a glass of wine, quietly adding some of the powder within and stirring it into the drink. She moved close to Angelica again, watching for the instant when she would set down her wine for a moment on one of the small tables around the room.

It was a matter of a few seconds at most, but Sophia had been waiting for it, and that made it easy to switch the wine. She walked away, sipping Angelica's drink, while the young noblewoman drank from the one Sophia had doctored.

It took a while to see any effect. For a minute or two, in fact, Sophia wasn't sure that she'd managed to do anything at all. Then she saw Angelica sway slightly, swatting away the attempt by one of her friends to help.

What's happening? Have I made some mistake?

Sophia saw her grab at her belt, searching for the now missing pouch. Angelica stumbled then, and this time one of her cronies did catch her. She looked as though she wanted to fight, or argue, but the whole coterie of them quickly swept her from the room, presumably looking for somewhere to rest.

Sophia smiled to herself at the thought that the other girl was getting what she deserved. She looked over at Sebastian.

Now for the part that *she* deserved.

Because the truth was, there was no one else in the room she had eyes for but him.

CHAPTER TEN

Kate felt worse off than she'd been before she got on the boat. She shivered as she walked through the city, the failing light nowhere near enough to dry out the soaking wet clothes she wore.

She was hungry too, so hungry that she was already contemplating theft to fill her rumbling stomach. Kate found herself looking around at every shop and food stall, searching for an opportunity, but there was no chance at the moment, even with her talent letting her spot when the coast was clear.

She almost found herself wishing she were back at the orphanage, but that was a stupid wish. Even before she'd run away, it had been a worse place than this. At least on the streets, there were no nuns to beat her for making mistakes, no endless hours of working at pointless tasks to avoid the sin of laziness.

This was close, though, and Kate found herself hoping that her sister was better off than this. Her attempts to connect with Sophia weren't working, though. Either that, or she was caught up with something that had her attention, so she couldn't answer. She tried to connect with Emeline again too. Again, there was no answer.

Kate kept walking.

She wasn't sure where she was in the city now, but from the look of it, she hadn't landed in some noble quarter. There, she imagined that the cobbles would be gleaming white marble, rather than cracked brick and granite covered in a layer of horse dung. The houses around her looked cheaper even than the ones around the House of the Unclaimed, and from inside them, Kate could hear occasional shouts and screams, arguments and laughter.

She passed by an inn, where the candlelight within lit up carousing barge hands and workers. The words of a bawdy song carried out onto the street, and in spite of herself Kate found herself blushing. One of the men beckoned to her, and Kate hurried on.

By daylight, Ashton had been a bustling, rough around the edges place. In the growing dark, this corner seemed a lot less friendly. In an alley nearby, Kate was sure that she heard the sounds of violence. As she passed another, she caught a man and a woman pressed up against a wall together and she looked away.

Kate knew that she had to get warmer than she was. In daylight, she might have been warm enough to dry out simply by walking around, but by night, with the moonlight streaming down on her in a haze of silver and the wind cutting through her whenever she didn't keep close to one of the walls?

She was going to freeze do death if she didn't find a fire.

There were fires all around the city in hearths and grates. The chimneys of the houses around her belched smoke into the night sky as their inhabitants cooked on them and kept warm. It wasn't as though she could just walk into one of their houses, though.

She could try an inn, but inns cost money, and if she just hung around one, Kate had no doubt that someone would want to know what she was doing there. So she kept walking, looking longingly at the inns nearby and trying to ignore the sounds of the city's more dangerous inhabitants as they went about their nocturnal business.

Finally, Kate felt as though she couldn't go on any longer. At the next inn she came to, she slipped into the courtyard it enclosed. She might not be able to pay for a room, but this one had a stable, and she might at least be able to keep warm there among the horses if she was careful. There would be stable hands somewhere, and the owners of the horses within would be out in the morning to take them. For now, though, Kate couldn't pick up any thoughts that would point to people being too close.

There were three horses in the stables at the moment. One was a dark stallion, large and aggressive looking. Another was a docile white pony that looked far too thin and poorly cared for. The third was a chestnut mare, which whickered as Kate moved close, slipping into her stall to huddle down among the straw. She took a blanket that was draped over the horse's back, and it didn't seem to mind when Kate wrapped herself in it.

It wasn't much, but it was far better than walking the street trying to dry out. She didn't try to sleep, because she didn't want to risk someone sneaking up on her while she did it. She just sat there while slowly, gradually, she started to warm up a little.

She also started to think. She had been planning to get out of the city when the boys had found her and she'd been forced to run. Her plan had been to steal everything she needed, from food to weapons, clothing to... well, a horse. Was there any reason she couldn't still do that?

Kate crept to the front of the stall, looking out while simultaneously extending her other senses. She had no illusions about what would happen to her if she was caught stealing something as expensive as a horse. It would be the branding iron at least, and more likely the noose.

But right then, when the alternative was dying a slow death in the city, it seemed more than worth the risk.

Actually doing it was the hard part. Kate could see some of the tack for a horse set on the wall, and the chestnut mare held still while Kate set her blanket in place and settled a saddle over the top. It was obviously used to strange people saddling it for its owner. She found more of the tack for it, and half-remembered lessons at the orphanage in how to be a good servant told her some of what she needed to know about where it all went. The rest, Kate guessed at, and when the horse didn't pull away from her efforts, she suspected that she had it right.

She opened the stable door as quietly as she could, every creak of the wood or squeak of the bolt sounding impossibly loud against the quiet of the night. She didn't dare to ride the horse from the stables, so instead, she led it quietly, step by step, until she reached the gate that led to the street.

"Hey, you! What do you think you're doing?"

Kate didn't hesitate. Her climb up into the saddle wasn't graceful, but it was fast. She dug her heels into the horse's flanks and yelled at the top of her voice. At the same time, she sent, as powerfully as she could, the urge to run.

Kate didn't know which aspect of it brought the horse to a gallop, but right then it didn't matter. The only thing that *did* matter was that she found herself clinging to the horse as it sprinted through the nighttime streets. Shouts sounded behind her, but they quickly faded into the distance.

The real difficulty was hanging onto the horse. Kate hadn't ridden before. The orphanage assumed that the only ones riding around her would be whoever bought her indenture. Certainly not her, and certainly not this fast.

That meant that she clung to the horse's neck for dear life, not even trying to steer it as it chose its own path past carts and the few pedestrians still out there. She hung on until the horse's strength started to fade, then pulled on the reins, trying to draw it to a halt.

She managed to slow it to a walk, at least, trying to orient herself. She didn't know exactly where she was in the city, but she had a sense of where the river was, because she'd pulled herself from it not that long ago. If she kept heading in the opposite direction, eventually, she would be out of the city.

Kate pointed the horse in what she hoped was the right direction and kept riding. She might not have ridden before, but she quickly found herself getting the rhythm of it, gripping with her legs and keeping going as her new mount took her past shops and inns, brothels and gambling parlors.

She passed one of the gaps in the old walls there. There had been a time when she would have had to ride through a closed off gate, getting past guards who would have wanted to know where she'd gotten the horse. Those days were long gone, though, the gates destroyed by cannon in one of the civil wars. Now, Kate was able to ride through with ease, traveling through into the greater quiet of the outer city.

There were still shouts somewhere behind her, but Kate doubted that anyone would be able to catch up now. Just to be sure, she kept off the main roads, so that anyone chasing would have to search for her. Out here, that meant going past rows of wooden buildings, most with their own small gardens to try to grow some extra food.

For the first time in her life, Kate felt truly free. She could just keep going, out into the Ridings with their open fields and their small villages, and no one would stop her. She would be able to find what she needed out there, whether it was food, or weapons, or just the freedom to live off the land.

She took a deep breath, resisting the urge to kick the horse into a gallop again. It had run hard enough for one night. For now, she wanted to keep going at a pace the chestnut could maintain until morning, so she let it continue its brisk walk through the outer reaches of the sprawling city.

It wasn't until she saw a blacksmith's shop that Kate drew her mount to a halt again. It was the one cluster of stone-built buildings in a sea of wood and clay brick construction, so solid looking that it seemed as though it had been there forever. There were examples of the owner's work out in the space around it, from wrought iron gates to scythes awaiting sharpening, to barrels of arrow shafts, just waiting for arrowheads to fit them.

Those caught Kate's attention. If there were arrowheads, there might be other things to go with them inside. There might be short hunting bows, just waiting for the kind of elaborate metal fittings some people loved. There might be knives. There might even be swords.

Kate knew that she ought to keep going. It would be safest not to risk any more thefts until she was clear of the city. Even the horse had been a massive risk. Yet it had been a risk that had left her far better off, hadn't it?

And maybe it was better to do this now, all in one go. People were already hunting for her, so maybe it was better to take all her risks tonight, rather than risking spoiling things once she was out in the open country. Somehow, Kate had the feeling that it was better to leave all her small crimes behind in the city once she left Ashton. This was still part of the life she was trying to leave behind; she didn't want to spoil her new life by making enemies in the villages out in the Ridings or the Shires beyond them.

Her mind made up, Kate hitched her horse to the fence around the side of the blacksmith's shop. She hopped over that fence, and the moment she had, it felt as though she'd done something irrevocable. She crept toward the blacksmith's shop, keeping low.

There were three buildings. One was clearly the main shop, another looked as though it might be the blacksmith's home, while the third was probably some kind of storage area and workshop. That was the one Kate slipped toward through the darkness, on the basis that it was the least likely to be tightly locked, and the most likely to contain completed weapons.

Sure enough, when Kate looked in through one of the tiny windows, she could see barrels with sword hilts and bows sticking from them, mixed in with ornamental ironwork and long nails designed for boat building.

Now, she just needed to find a way in. Kate made her way around to the door, but there was a large, wrought iron lock on that and the handle wouldn't move when she tried it. She moved back around to the window, eyeing the leaded glass there. Would she fit through? It would be a tight fit, but Kate thought that she might make it.

She would have to break the window to do it, but with so many objects scattered around the yard, that proved to be easy. She just picked up a twisted iron railing spike and swung.

The glass breaking sounded far too loud against the silence, and Kate held still, listening for activity. When there was none, she knocked out the rest of the glass and pulled herself through the window.

Kate searched through the barrels. She didn't know as much about weapons as she wanted to, but Kate could see that some of the creations here were better than others. There were some swords that seemed light and springy, while others seemed like cheap copies of them. Even some of the blades with more elaborate-looking hilts had blades without any flex, and with just a dull shine to them rather than the wave patterned metal of the better ones.

The same went for the bows. Some were just straight yew and ash, while others seemed to be composites of many layers of wood and horn, bound with metal. Kate took the best she could find. If she was going to do this, she was going to do it right. There was no way that she could climb out of the window again with them strapped to her, so she tossed them out ahead of her, then climbed back through, tumbling to the ground in the darkness and coming up to a crouch.

A hand closed over her shoulder, large enough and strong enough that Kate had no chance of escape. She spun, trying to pull away, and strong arms wrapped around her.

Kate swallowed, knowing she was finished.

CHAPTER ELEVEN

Sophia forced herself to stand and watch the ball as the dancing started, groups of people moving through formal court dances that she simply didn't know the steps to. She wanted to rush forward in the direction of Prince Sebastian, but right then, it was hard to get her feet moving in the right direction.

What did you come here for, then? Sophia asked herself.

That was the question. She couldn't be timid about this. If she couldn't bring herself to even talk to the prince, then she had to make her way over to one of the other men in the room. If she couldn't do that, then she needed to leave, sell what she had, and hope that it would be enough to keep her off the streets for a night or two.

Wasn't it better to go over to the prince than to do either of those things? Wasn't it better to just talk to a young man she liked? Sophia found herself able to move again with that thought, and she started to pick her way through the crowd.

Not everyone was dancing, even now. The older nobles there mostly watched from the sidelines, talking to one another about whose son or daughter or niece was dancing the most elegantly, about the wars across the Knife-Water, about the latest artists patronized by the dowager or the fact that Lord Horrige's daughter had elected to become a nun of the Masked Goddess. Just the mention of it was enough to steer Sophia away from the conversation.

She kept drifting toward the prince. He wasn't dancing yet, although his brother was, swapping from partner to partner with the laughing ebullience of a man who knew he could have his pick of the women. Sophia made sure that she avoided *him*. She had no interest in being swept up in the whirl of his amusement.

As she stepped out toward Prince Sebastian, she was sure she caught him looking her way. It was hard to tell for sure with the mask obscuring his expression, but her talent seemed to catch his surprise.

She's coming over to me? I assumed a girl that lovely would have a full dance card already.

"Your Highness," Sophia said as she reached him, curtseying because they'd taught the girls how to do that much at least at the

House of the Unclaimed. "I hope you don't mind me coming over like this."

Mind? Only if she's going to start going on about how perfect the ball is. I hate how contrived these things are.

"No, I don't mind," he said. "I'm sorry, I can't guess who's under that mask."

"Sophia of Meinhalt," she said, remembering her false identity. "I'm sorry, I'm not very good at parties. I'm not sure what I should be doing."

"I'm not very good at them either," Sebastian admitted.

They're meat markets.

"You don't have to hide from me," Sophia said. "I can see you don't like them much. Is it too many people looking for advantage in one place?" She paused. "I'm sorry, that was too forward of me. If you want me to go—"

Sebastian reached out for her arm. "Please don't. It's refreshing to meet someone who is prepared to be honest about what's happening here."

Sophia actually felt a little guilty about that, since she was more than aware that she was there under false pretenses. At the same time, she felt more of a connection to Sebastian as he stood next to her than to any of the others there. He felt real while so many of the others seemed like simple facades.

The truth was that she liked him, and it seemed as though he liked her. Sophia could see his thoughts as clearly as fish at the bottom of a river. They were bright things, without the edge of cruelty to them that his brother's had. More than that, she could see how he felt and thought when he looked at her.

"Why did you come to the ball if you hate them so much?" Sophia asked. "I'd have thought a prince could choose not to."

Sebastian shook his head. "Maybe it works that way in Meinhalt. Here, it's all duty. My mother wishes me to attend, and so I attend."

"She's probably hoping you'll meet a nice girl," Sophia said. She looked around pointedly. "I'm sure there must be one somewhere."

She managed to get him to laugh with that.

"I thought I just had," Sebastian countered. He seemed to realize what he'd just said. "What about you, Sophia? Why are you at this ball?"

Sophia found that she didn't want to lie to him on that; at least, not any more than she had to.

"I didn't have anywhere else to go," she said, and Sebastian must have heard the sadness there. Obviously, he couldn't know the reason for it, but even if he thought that this was about some foreign noble who'd had to run from the wars, the sympathy in his next words mattered.

"I'm sorry. I didn't mean to bring up difficult subjects," Sebastian said. He offered her his hand. "Would you like to dance?"

Sophia took it, surprised to find that there was nothing she wanted more right then. "I'd like to."

They moved out toward the dance floor together. It occurred to Sophia then that there was one obvious problem with doing so.

"I should probably warn you that I'm not the best dancer. I don't even know the steps to all the dances here."

She saw Sebastian smile. "At least you have the excuse of a whole different set of court dances out in Meinhalt. I'm simply not very good, and I've had tutors tell me that, so it must be true."

Sophia put a hand on his arm. She knew firsthand what it was like to have cruel teachers. She doubted that any of the prince's had beaten him, but there were ways to be cruel without ever laying a finger on someone.

"That's a horrible thing to say to someone," she said. "I'm sure you dance better than you think."

"At the very least, we can learn together," Sebastian said.

For the first couple of steps of the new dance, Sophia faltered, not knowing what to do. Then the obvious occurred to her: there was a whole room full of people around her who *did* know the steps to the dance, and who would have to think about them in order to be able to execute them.

She listened using her power, hoping that it would pick up everything she needed, using her eyes to catch the rest as she watched the rhythms of the other dancers. One girl a little way away seemed to be thinking her way through the steps with the concentration of someone who had been drilled in them by a dance tutor not too long ago.

"You're picking this up quickly," Sebastian said as Sophia started to move.

"You're not doing too badly yourself," she assured him.

He wasn't. In spite of his assertions that he couldn't dance well, the only problem Sophia could see with Sebastian's dancing was a kind of self-conscious stiffness. That seemed to come and go, depending on whether he remembered that people were watching him, so Sophia decided to distract him.

"Tell me about yourself," she said as they whirled among the other couples there.

"What's to tell?" Sebastian answered. "I'm the younger son of the dowager, technically lord of a minor duchy out in the west, and largely unimportant as far as the succession goes. I do whatever duty requires of me, which includes attending balls."

Sophia brushed her hand across his shoulder. "I'm glad you did. But I'm not interested in all that. I want to know about *you*. What makes you smile? What do you like most in the world? When you're with friends, do they treat you like you're still a prince, or are you just Sebastian to them?"

Sebastian was quiet for so long that Sophia suspected that she'd gotten it wrong in spite of the advantages her powers gave her.

"I don't know," he said at last. "I'm not sure if I have friends, not really. At best, I've always been the one on the edge of my brother's social group. Faced with most of them, maybe that isn't such a bad thing. In any case, my one job as a younger prince is not to be embarrassing. That's easier if I avoid the kind of entanglements Rupert generates. And to be honest, books are more interesting than most of them."

Sophia held him a little closer. "It sounds lonely. I hope that I'm more interesting than a book, at least."

"A lot more interesting," Sebastian said, and then seemed to realize what he'd said. "I'm sorry, I shouldn't..."

Even if it's true.

"It's all right," Sophia said. She could see his embarrassment at overstepping, but her talent showed her how glad he was that she didn't mind, and what he was starting to think every time he looked at her. It was strange, seeing the room seem to light up for someone just because Sophia was there.

Sebastian looked as though he might be about to say something else, but another girl chose that moment to come up to them, her arm out as if to ask him to dance. Sophia could see how that would play out, with the prince passed from one lovely girl to another, completely forgetting about her.

To her surprise, though, Sebastian took a step back from the girl.

"Perhaps later," he said, although he did it gently. "As you can see, I have a partner for this dance."

"I have my dance card—" the girl began, but Sophia was already dancing with Sebastian in the opposite direction.

She needn't have worried. Sebastian's eyes were solely on her as they kept dancing. Sophia loved his voice as he talked about the things that excited him, not the petty wars most noblemen might have been interested in, but art and the world, the people of the city and the things he was able to do as a prince to make things better.

"Of course," he said, "it's not like the days before the civil wars, when kings and queens could just do what they wanted. Now, everything goes through the Assembly of Nobles."

"Leaving you feeling as though you can't do any good?" Sophia guessed.

Sebastian nodded.

"Ashton is a cruel city," he said, "and the rest of the country isn't much better. Worse, in some of the more lawless parts. It would be good to be able to help."

Sophia had always assumed that nobles just spat on those below them, not caring about how harsh their lives were. When it came to Sebastian, at least, it seemed that she was wrong.

Even so, she didn't want to tell him the truth about who she was. Right then, the moment felt too precious for that. It felt as fine spun as a cobweb, and as fragile. One wrong move and it might all fall apart.

Sophia didn't want it to fall apart. She liked Sebastian, and one look at his thoughts told her that he more than liked her. Right then, it felt as though she could stay and dance with him, talk with him, all night.

So she did.

She spun in Sebastian's arms as another song played. She talked to him about life in the palace, about the places he'd seen and the people he'd spoken to. She drew out the parts of him that shone like diamonds in his thoughts, drawing him away from the mundane days and the pressures of court life.

When it came to Sophia's own life, she kept things as general as she could. She could admit to having a sister, but couldn't tell him stories about their lives except in the vaguest of details, because that would have meant talking about the orphanage. She could only keep up with mentions of the latest news because she could lift the details from the prince's mind. The best she could do was to steer the conversation back to Sebastian, or talk about things that wouldn't give away where she'd come from, or what she'd done to get there.

At some point in that, it simply seemed natural that she should kiss him. Sophia stepped back for a moment, then leaned in deliberately closer, ignoring the looks of some of the young noblewomen at the sides of the room. This wasn't about them. It was about her, and Sebastian, and—

When the clocks struck, the clamor of their bells cut through the music, and through whatever had bound Sophia to Sebastian all evening. The shock of it made them both glance away, and in that moment, whatever had been about to pull them into a kiss shattered.

Sophia looked up to see some of those around the edges watching the two of them, talking in low tones. The younger women definitely didn't look happy as they started to drift away, taking off their masks as they went.

"Is the party done?" Sophia asked. "It... it doesn't seem an hour since it started."

"Three," Sebastian said, but only after a glance at a reflected clock face to confirm it. Sophia could see that the time had flown past for him as well. "It's a strange feeling. Normally, these things seem to stretch out for an eternity."

"It must be the company," Sophia said with a smile.

"I think it probably is," Sebastian said. He took off his mask then, and if Sophia's heart hadn't already been beating hard at the thought of him, it would have done then. He was handsomer than she'd thought, not plain and forgettable compared to his brother, as he'd seemed in the thoughts of so many others.

"May I?" Sebastian asked, reaching up for her mask. "It's bad luck to keep a mask on after the end of a masque, and they'll think you don't know our ways if you wear it back to your carriage."

Sophia felt a moment of fear then. Behind her mask, she was Sophia of Meinhalt, a stranger who couldn't be identified. Without it... would she be enough?

She felt Sebastian's fingers as they delicately removed the half mask that she hid behind. He looked at her then, and Sophia could hear his thoughts as clearly as if he'd shouted them.

Goddess, she is even more perfect than I could have believed! Is this... is this what love feels like?

Sophia was asking herself the same question, and that brought a problem with it. Sophia tried to bury that as Sebastian started to walk her back out toward the front of the palace, gliding with her among the crowds of people.

Sophia could see some of the girls there watching her with barely disguised hostility.

Who is she? What is she doing here?

Sophia could feel their anger at not being the ones on the prince's arm, but right then, she only wanted to concentrate on Sebastian.

"When will I see you again?" Sebastian asked.

Sophia wasn't sure what to say to that. How could she answer it, when the only reason she'd gotten in there at all was a lie? The great flaw in her plan gaped in front of her then: it gained her entrance to the palace once, but it gave her nothing beyond that. It showed her this world and then shut her off from it.

Sebastian reached up to touch her face.

"What is it?"

Sophia hadn't thought that her worry would show so clearly. She thought as quickly as she could.

"The carriage awaiting me..." she began, trying so hard not to lie but knowing she had no choice, "...it will take me back to..."

"The ship?" he offered, concern in his face. "Back home, across the sea?"

She nodded, relieved he said it and that she didn't have to utter the lie.

"It would," she said, "and yet...I have no home, not really," she said. "My home is not what it was. It is all in ruins." That part, at least, was easy to fake, as there was some truth in it. "I sailed across the waters to escape my home. I am loath to return. Especially so soon after meeting you."

She saw confusion cross Sebastian's face, and then determination.

"Stay here," Sebastian said. "This is a palace. There are more guest rooms than I can count."

Sophia didn't answer. She found that she didn't want to lie to him more than she had to. That was a foolish thing, when every inch of her was a lie right then, but still, Sophia didn't want to say the words.

"You're offering to let me stay?" she said. "Just like that?"

Sophia could barely believe that. Sebastian filled the gap, and it turned out that he only needed two words to do it, holding out a hand to her as the last of the others filed from the hall.

"Stay?" he asked again.

Sophia reached out and took his waiting hand and, slowly, she smiled.

"There is nothing I would love more," she said.

CHAPTER TWELVE

Kate winced as the blacksmith hammered a loop of chain closed around her wrist, anchoring her to the wrought iron fence. Kate tried to pull her hand free, but there was no give in the metal.

There didn't seem to be much give in the man who'd forged it, either. He seemed as strong as the iron he worked with, barrel-chested and powerful. His wife was narrow featured and worried looking.

"That's it, Thomas? You're just going to leave her where she might get free?"

"Easy, Winifred," the smith said. "The girl won't get free. I know my work."

His wife still didn't seem convinced. She should have tried being where Kate was. Right then, it felt as though a vise was clamped around her wrist. She wanted to lash out, to fight, but the weapons she'd stolen were gone, and she couldn't even get free.

"She's little better than an animal," the woman said. "We should hand her over to a magistrate, Thomas, before she murders us all."

"She isn't going to murder us," the smith said, shaking his head at the drama of it all. "And if we hand her over to a magistrate, they'll hang her. She's barely more than a girl. Do you want to be responsible for her being hanged?"

Fear crept into Kate at that thought. She'd known the risks of stealing while she'd done it, but knowing them was a different thing from the threat that her death might actually happen. She did her best to look as innocent and harmless as possible. Kate wasn't sure that she was any good at it. It was the kind of thing Sophia had always been better at. Sometimes, in the orphanage, she'd been able to keep from being beaten just because the masked sisters there had liked her.

Not very often, though. The House of the Unclaimed had been a harsh place, after all.

"I'm sorry," Kate said.

"I hardly believe *that*," the blacksmith's wife snapped. "There's a horse there that I doubt she came by honestly, and she was stealing *weapons*. Why would a girl like this want weapons? What was she planning to do? Become a bandit?"

What if they see the horse? What if they think we're harboring a thief?

Kate could see the woman's fears were more about what would happen if they didn't hand Kate over, rather than a real hatred of her.

"I wasn't going to be a bandit," Kate said. "I was going to live free and hunt my food."

"Being a poacher is *better*?" Winifred demanded. "This is foolishness. Do what you want, Thomas, but I'm going back into the house."

She made good on her declaration, stalking back toward the main building. The smith watched her go, and Kate took the opportunity to try to escape again. It didn't make any difference.

"You might as well stop trying," the smith said. "I forge my metal well."

"I could call out for help," Kate said. "I could tell people that you kidnapped me, and you're holding me here against my will."

She saw the big man spread his hands. "I would show them the broken window, the things you tried to steal. Then you *would* be looking at the magistrate."

Kate guessed that was true. The blacksmith was probably at the heart of the community in this small section of the city, while she was a girl who had appeared off the street. Then there was the horse, and the people who would know that she had stolen it.

"That's better," Thomas said. "Maybe we can talk now. Who are you? Do you have a name?"

"Kate," she said. She found that she couldn't look straight at him then. She actually felt ashamed by all this, and that was something Kate hadn't thought she would feel.

"Well, Kate, I'm Thomas." His voice was kinder than Kate had expected. "Now, where have you come from?"

Kate shrugged. "Does it matter?"

"It matters if you have a family looking for you. Parents."

Kate snorted at that idea. Her parents were long gone, lost in a night that… she shook her head. It refused to come to her even now. Sophia might know, but Sophia wasn't there.

"Which leaves several possibilities," Thomas said. He grabbed at the leg of her stolen trousers, lifting it to reveal the tattoo that marked her as one of the Unclaimed. Kate squirmed away from his grip, but by then it was too late.

"Are you running away from your indenture?" Thomas asked. He shook his head. "No, you're too young. From one of the orphanages then? You have hunters after you?"

"They sent some of the boys from the orphanage," Kate admitted.

She tried to read the blacksmith then, and work out what he was going to do next. If he handed her back, she had no doubt that there would be some kind of reward for him, and in her experience, people did whatever was in their own best interest. She reached out for his mind, and she found him staring back at her.

"You're one of them, aren't you?" Thomas said.

"What do you mean?" Kate countered. She knew from painful experience that anyone who knew what she was would react badly. Hadn't the barge hands thrown her into the river to drown because of it?

She saw Thomas shake his head. "There's no point in trying to hide it. One of our neighbor's sons... he was like you. He always seemed to know what we were thinking, even when we didn't say it. I learned to get a feel for when he was listening in. We didn't know what he was until we heard some of the masked priests giving their sermons."

"I don't know... I don't know what you're talking about," Kate said.

Thomas reached out, unchaining her wrist.

"You can run if you want," he said, "but I'm not going to hurt you."

Kate didn't run. She had the feeling that the blacksmith had more he wanted to say.

He did. "I don't care about what you're able to do. As far as I'm concerned, you aren't cursed, or evil, or anything else they say. Listen... my son Will has gone off to one of the companies. Wants to be a great soldier. Well, I've needed help around the forge ever since."

Kate frowned at that, trying to understand what the blacksmith was saying.

"You're offering me a job?"

It wasn't what she'd escaped from the House of the Unclaimed for. It wasn't what she'd wanted when she'd been trying to leave the city, either. Yet she had to admit that there was something enticing about the prospect.

"You're running," Thomas said. "But my guess is that you don't have much of a plan. They chase the indentured who run. If they catch you, they'll hurt you, and then they'll sell you on. This way, you get to work at something I guess you'd like. You get to be safe, and I get help. You can have food and shelter, learn my trade." He looked at Kate expectantly. "What do you say?"

Kate hadn't expected this when he'd caught her. She hadn't expected anything but violence, and probably the hangman's rope. She felt as if it was all happening far too quickly, leaving her reeling.

He was right though. She would be safe like this, and she would be learning something she wanted to know how to do. She wouldn't be in the country, but maybe there would be time for that in the future.

"Where do we start?" she asked.

**

The smithy was a dark space as they walked in, and Kate felt a hint of worry as she felt Thomas's hand on her shoulder, guiding her in. What if this was all some kind of trick? For what, though? Kate couldn't imagine what he might want.

He would want something. Everyone wanted *something*.

She waited while he lit a lamp, then moved over to the forge, laying out charcoal in something that looked far more careful than just a random mixture.

"Watch carefully," he said. "One of your jobs will be to help light the forge in the morning, and there's an art to doing it well."

Kate watched the patterns of it, trying to make sense of it.

"Why do it that way?" she asked. "Why not just throw the charcoal in?"

She saw Thomas shrug. "Heat is a blacksmith's greatest tool. It must be treated with care. Too much fuel, or too little, too much air or too little, all of this can ruin iron."

Kate was surprised when he handed her a flint and steel, pointing to a spot where he'd set kindling.

"We start with wood, then build."

Kate set to work with the flint and steel, striking sparks until the flames flickered in the kindling.

"Why did you run away?" Thomas asked.

"Do you know what the orphanage is like?" Kate countered. It was difficult to keep a hard edge out of her voice at the thought of it.

"I wasn't there, so I would guess not," the smith said. "I've heard rumors."

Rumors. Those weren't the same as the real thing. They weren't even close. A rumor was a few words, quickly forgotten. The reality had been pain and violence and fear. It had been a place where every day had involved being told she was less than everyone else, and that she should be grateful just for the chance to be told it.

"It was that bad then?" Thomas asked, and it was only as he said it that Kate guessed how much of it must have shown on her face.

"It was that bad," Kate agreed.

"Aye, there are some evil places in this world," Thomas said. "And they're often not where the priests tell us they are." He nodded in the direction of a large set of bellows. "I'll work you hard here, Kate, if you want to stay. Let's see if you can get some air into the fire so it gets hot enough."

Kate went to the bellows, expecting them to move easily. Instead, it was as hard as one of the cranks of the grinding wheels at the orphanage had been. The difference was that, as she strained at the bellows, she could see them making a difference. The forge fire grew, changing color as she fed it with air and charcoal. She watched the flames shift from yellow to orange, to a white heat that could move steel.

Thomas took a piece of iron, placing it within the forge. "Keep going, Kate. Iron only shifts slowly. There are things we can't rush."

He said it with the patience of someone who had worked a lot of the metal. Kate kept working, ignoring the sweat building up on her skin. She found herself wanting to impress the smith. After what he'd offered her, she wanted to show him that she was worth it. It was a strange feeling; at the orphanage, she hadn't cared. Maybe that was just because they hadn't cared about her, except as a commodity.

"See the shade the iron has gone?" Thomas asked. "When we get the metal out of the forge, we'll have to work it quickly. When it starts to fade, we have to get it back in the forge."

Kate understood, and she rushed to grab a pair of tongs, reaching for the metal and snatching it out at speed. She didn't want to waste a single instant in her forging. The movement was too quick, and Kate felt the moment when the metal slipped and twisted from her grip, falling to the stone floor of the forge.

It brushed her leg on the way down, and Kate screamed. White heat flashed through her, the barest brush of it pure agony. Thomas was there in an instant, tipping a trough of water over her and the metal both. Kate heard the metal cracking, but right then, there was no time to care. It simply hurt too much.

"Hold still," Thomas said, grabbing a jar of pungent salve. It proved to be gentle and cooling, numbing Kate's leg so that the

75

agony receded. From where she lay, Kate could see the cracks in the billet of iron she'd grabbed too quickly.

"I'm sorry," she said. She waited for Thomas to hit her for her clumsiness, the way the nuns would have. Instead, he held out a hand, lifting her up.

"The main thing is that you're not hurt worse," he said. "It's a bad burn, but it will heal."

"But the iron…" Kate began.

Thomas waved that away. "Iron cracks. The important thing is that you learn to be patient. You can't become a master smith in one day, or even in a hundred. You can't rush around a forge. It's a place for patience and calm, because the alternative is burnt skin and broken metal."

"I'll do better," Kate insisted.

He nodded. "I know you will."

CHAPTER THIRTEEN

Sophia walked beside Sebastian, heading deeper into the palace with him. She found her hand creeping into his as they walked, her delicate fingers interlacing with his much stronger ones. She had never thought that such a simple moment of human contact could feel so important.

"Why did you agree to dance with me?" Sophia asked.

Sebastian looked at her as if he didn't understand. "You sound surprised."

"Shouldn't I be?" she said with a tilt of her head. "I mean, I'm no one, not really. And you're... well, *you*."

That was probably closer to the reality of it all than Sophia should have gone, but right then it was hard to keep from saying more than she meant. She might have gone to the ball with the intention of doing something like this, but the thought that she might succeed with someone as kind and as good and as handsome as Sebastian was more than she could have hoped.

She's more amazing than anyone I've met, and she's wondering why I wanted to dance with her?

Sophia smiled as she caught that thought, although she didn't say anything about it. She imagined that nothing would ruin the mood quite so quickly as letting Sebastian know what she really was.

"I'm just glad that *you* agreed to dance with *me*," Sebastian said, as if he weren't a prince, or handsome, or everything that Sophia imagined anyone could want. Did he really not know it? No, Sophia could see that he didn't, and in its way that only made him more desirable.

Sophia had gone there with the intention of seducing someone, but now she was starting to think that those things cut both ways.

That thought brought with it a sense of nervousness that Sophia hadn't expected to feel, even as she looked at Sebastian, imagining the play of the muscles under his clothing. She felt a little guilty too, because everything she was in that moment was a lie, and because of everything she'd gone there to do.

It seemed so cynical now, going to the court to snare the attentions of some rich man, or inveigle her way into the good graces of some noble friend. Compared to what she was feeling now, that all felt cheap and tawdry.

"What are you thinking?" Sebastian asked, reaching up to touch her face. Sophia had a brief moment to reflect that it must be strange, living your life having to ask that. Mostly though, she thought about how perfect his skin felt against hers.

"Just that I still can't quite believe this is happening," Sophia said. "I mean... I have nothing. I *am* nothing."

She saw Sebastian shake his head. "Don't ever say that. The war might have taken your home, but you're still... you're amazing, Sophia. I saw you at the party, and it was like you were the sun standing among dim stars."

"Wasn't it your brother who was supposed to be the sun?" Sophia joked, but then put a hand on Sebastian's arm to stop him as he started to answer. Partly because she didn't want to go there, and partly because she could feel that Sebastian didn't either. "No, don't. I don't want to talk about Prince Rupert. I'd rather hear about you."

Sebastian actually laughed then. "Normally, it's the other way around. The number of times I've had women come up to me just because they want to get closer to my brother, you'd think I was his pimp or his procurer."

Sophia could feel the note of bitterness there. She guessed that it was hard being the brother no one paid any attention to. They kept walking along corridors lined with wood panels and hunting trophies, every niche hung with tapestries and paintings that made Sophia want to stop and stare at the sheer quality of the work involved.

"I find it hard to believe that women would ignore you," Sophia said. "Are they blind?"

It was too much, but right then, she couldn't help herself.

"There are some," Sebastian admitted. "They crowd around sometimes, and I can see them planning who will make the next move."

"Milady d'Angelica?" Sophia asked.

That brought a smile. "Among others."

Sophia couldn't help herself then. "She *is* very beautiful. And I'm told she has excellent taste in dresses."

That earned her a small look of puzzlement, but that was quickly gone.

"I guess I'm looking for more than that," Sebastian said. "And... well, I get the feeling that they're hoping to catch me in a marriage. I want to be more to someone than just the object in a game."

The guilt from before flashed through Sophia again then, because in her way, she was every bit as bad as the others were. Well, maybe not as bad as a girl who had been planning to drug Sebastian and take advantage of that, but she was still being anything but honest with him.

"I wish I could say that my intentions were entirely pure," Sophia said. She shouldn't be warning the prince, but right then she felt as though she owed it to him. She could see what kind of man he was. Exactly the kind of honesty and kindness that made him so attractive to her meant that Sophia felt as though she shouldn't be doing this at all. "I wish that this were *just* because I liked you."

"But you do like me?" Sebastian said.

There was no one else around right then, so Sophia let herself do what she'd wanted to do since the ballroom, and kissed him.

It was a strange experience. The only time it had happened in the orphanage had been when an older boy had pushed Sophia up against a wall, forcing his mouth against hers until one of the nuns had broken it up. Sophia had been beaten for it, as if she'd had any choice in it all. That had been rough, and brief, and disgusting.

This kiss was none of those things. Sebastian, it turned out, was a gentle kisser, whose mouth met Sophia's in what seemed like a perfect joining of two halves into one whole. Sophia could sense the concern in him, not wanting to drive her away even as he wanted to kiss her deeper. She wrapped her arms around him, encouraging him, and for a moment or two, Sophia let herself be swept away by it.

"I hope that answers your question," Sophia said. "It's just—"

"That you *are* homeless, and you *do* need to do what it takes for a noble girl to survive?" Sebastian suggested. "I understand, Sophia. Let's face it, most of the girls in there wouldn't have been half so honest."

Probably not, Sophia guessed, but right then, she didn't want Sebastian thinking about the other girls who had been in the ballroom.

"Are we okay?" she asked. She hadn't thought it would be this hard to bring herself to seduce someone. Maybe she should have gone with someone else. Someone she could have done this to without feeling guilty.

The truth was that Sophia didn't want anyone else.

"I think we're more than okay," Sebastian said, offering her his arm.

Sophia took it, relishing the feeling of being that close to him. It made her heart beat a little faster just to be there, and she found herself missing half of the beautiful things they passed in the palace, simply because she spent her time staring at Sebastian instead.

The palace was impressive, though. It seemed to stretch forever, in washes of marble and gold that must have cost a fortune to construct.

"It must have been incredible, growing up in a place like this," Sophia said, thinking of just how different it all was from the orphanage. There was the most precious thing of all here: space. Space without people shouting or giving her orders. Space without a hundred other girls all forced into hating one another because they had to compete for every scrap of kindness and food.

"It's an impressive building," Sebastian said, "but honestly, it isn't the one I spent the most time in as a child. My mother had me raised on one of the smaller country estates we own, because there were times when the city seemed too dangerous."

Sophia hadn't thought about that. Of course the dowager would have a dozen castles and homes spread around the kingdom.

"It was just you?" Sophia asked. "Not you and your brother, or you with your mother?" She caught a hint of sadness in Sebastian's thoughts then, and reached up to brush his jaw with her fingers. "I'm sorry, I didn't mean to ruin the mood."

"No, it's fine," Sebastian replied. "It's actually good to have someone who wants to know. But no, I was mostly kept apart from Rupert, and from Mother. The idea was that we wouldn't all be in the same place if anything... happened."

In other words, so that one of them would survive if there was an attack or a fire, a plague or some other disaster. Sophia could understand it in a way, but even so, it seemed like a harsh way to live. Kate had been the only one giving her the strength to keep going when they'd been younger.

"Well, I'm glad you're here now," Sophia said.

"So am I," Sebastian assured her.

They made their way up to a suite of rooms shut off from the rest of the palace by a solid oak door. Sophia had been expecting a bedroom beyond, but instead, it was like a whole house crammed into the space. There was a receiving room furnished with older but comfortable divans and rugs, and there were doors leading off the space that Sophia guessed led to bedrooms or dressing rooms.

Sebastian held her out at arm's length. "Sophia, there's a second bedroom here if you want it. I... I don't want you to feel that you have to do anything, just to get my help."

That was one of the kindest things anyone had done for Sophia. She'd assumed that everyone wanted something. She'd assumed that even for nobles, safety was a kind of transaction. Yet here the prince was, giving her a chance to get everything she wanted without having to ever go near his bed.

"You're a good man, Sebastian," she said, taking his hands. "A kind man."

She kissed his hands, then pulled him closer.

"And that's why I *don't* just want to sleep in the room next door."

They kissed again then, and there was far more passion in this attempt than there had been in the previous one. Perhaps part of that was that Sophia had far more confidence that she knew what to do now. Perhaps part of it was that Sebastian didn't feel as though he had to hold back.

They clung to each other, kissing as their hands started to explore one another. Sophia felt a moment of nervousness then, and Sebastian looked at her.

"Are you all right?" he asked.

She nodded. "It's just... I haven't—"

"I understand," Sebastian said. "You don't need to be afraid of me, though."

Sophia kissed him again. "I'm not."

Somehow, between them, they made their way across the floor of the reception room without ever letting go of one another. Sophia fumbled with the stays of her dress, then gasped as Sebastian started to undo them for her.

He pushed open the door to one of the rooms there, and Sophia got a glimpse of a four-poster bed in blue silk before Sebastian lifted her, laying her down on it as gently as a feather.

"Yes?" he asked.

Sophia smiled up at him. "Yes, Sebastian. Very much yes."

***

Afterward, Sophia lay in the dark, curled against Sebastian and listening to his breathing as he slept. She could feel the press of his muscles against her back there, and the movement as he shifted in his sleep made her want to wake him and start everything they'd finished again.

She didn't, though, even though everything that had gone before had been more beautiful, more pleasurable, just... more, than she could have ever imagined. She wanted to take everything she could now, but the truth was that Sophia hoped that there would be time enough not to have to. She hoped that there would be a dozen more nights like this, a hundred.

A lifetime's worth.

She felt the weight of his arm draped over her in sleep, and right then, Sophia felt as though she had everything she could ever have wanted.

CHAPTER FOURTEEN

The morning came, and when it did, Kate wasn't sure that she'd ever worked so hard in her life. Not on any of the orphanage's wheels or chores, certainly not since. The strangest part of it was that she was happier than she'd ever been too. Happy to be doing this work, pounding metal and working the bellows.

It helped that Thomas was a patient teacher. Where they'd beaten her at the orphanage, he corrected Kate by showing her better ways to do things and reminding her when she forgot.

"We need to draw out the metal more," he said. "With a scythe blade, it needs to be thin and sharp. It needs slicing, not impact."

Kate nodded, helping to hold the billet in place while he struck it, then pumping the bellows to get the flames to the correct temperature. There was so much to learn around the forge, so many little subtleties that went beyond simply heating metal and hitting it. Already today, she'd learned about the art of welding metal together in the forge, about the scale that formed with too much work on iron, and about judging the difference between good iron and bad.

"I want to cover the back half of the blade with clay when we harden it," Thomas said, "because...?"

"Because that will mean it cools slower than the edge?" Kate guessed.

"Very good," Thomas said. "That will mean that the edge is harder, while the rest is less brittle. You're doing well, Kate."

Kate wasn't sure that she'd ever had anyone encourage her before. In her life to date, there had only been punishments when she'd done something wrong.

Some lessons were easier than others. Metalwork required patience that Kate hadn't built up. She always wanted to do the next thing, when sometimes the only thing to do was wait while metal heated up or cooled down.

"There are things you can't rush," Thomas said. "You have time, Kate. Savor your life, don't wish away the moments."

Kate did her best, but even so, it wasn't easy. Now that she'd found something she enjoyed doing, she didn't want to waste a moment of it. There *were* plenty of wasted moments, though, mostly spent looking through the forge or the shed nearby for things they needed. Despite Thomas's obvious talents as a smith, organization clearly wasn't one of them.

"I'll go and fetch lunch for us," Thomas said. "Winifred has been making bread. Don't try to forge anything yourself while I'm gone."

He left for the house, and Kate found herself chafing under the weight of his instruction. If he hadn't told her not to do it, she probably *would* have jumped up and started working on a knife or a section of wrought iron. Probably a knife, because Kate could see the usefulness of that in a way that she couldn't with a decorative bracket or a gate bar.

She couldn't just stand still, though, couldn't just rest, in spite of the heat and the closeness of the forge. In the absence of anything better to do, Kate found herself starting to reorganize things. The tongs made no sense in a random tangle of ironwork, so Kate hung them up on a hook. The sections of metal made no sense in a rough pile that made no distinction between brass and iron, hard steel and mild.

Kate started to sort through it all, arranging it into neat stacks. She set the tools in places that seemed to make sense, based on where Thomas would probably need them. From the forge, she went over to the shed, with its barrels and its stacks, setting everything into place, trying to bring some kind of order to the chaos of it all.

It took a while, but Kate could see how to do it. She pictured herself moving through the shed and the forge, picking things up as she needed them. Then she simply put things where they needed to be in order to make that work. She swept the floor, tidying away the fragments of metal that had fallen there, and the sand that had spilled from casting in brass and bronze.

"You look as though you've been busy," Thomas said as he came back.

In that moment, fear crept into Kate's heart. What if she'd done the wrong thing? What if he punished her for it? What if he told her to leave, and Kate found herself having to find her way on the streets of Ashton again? She wasn't sure that she could go back to that, so soon after having found a place in which to be safe.

"You aren't angry, are you?" Kate asked.

"Angry?" Thomas said with a laugh. "I've been meaning to organize this place for years. Winifred keeps telling me to do it, but what with one thing and another... well, I've never gotten around to it. It looks as though you've done a good job, too."

Thomas handed her half a loaf then, stuffed with cheese and ham. It was more food than Kate was used to being given in the orphanage, and certainly more than she'd managed to steal for herself on the streets. She wanted to think that there had been a time as a child when she had been well fed and cared for, but the truth was that Kate couldn't remember it. It was hard to believe that it could possibly all be for her.

Even so, Kate ate, because she wasn't going to let food go to waste. Especially not since she was starving after working the forge so long. She devoured the bread at a speed that made Thomas raise an eyebrow.

"I hadn't realized you were that hungry, or we'd have stopped sooner."

Kate wiped her mouth, realized that she probably didn't look very civilized right then, and didn't care. That was something that her sister might have worried about, but it wasn't something for her to be concerned with.

She looked around, and found herself hoping that Sophia had found something as good as this for herself. Kate wasn't sure if this would last forever, because she couldn't imagine anything lasting forever right then, but if it did, she wouldn't mind. This was as close to perfect as she could have hoped for.

When she was done with her lunch, it seemed that Thomas had more lessons for her.

"You want to know about weapons more than the rest of it, don't you?" he asked.

Kate nodded.

"Before you can forge them, you need to know about the differences between them. Come with me."

He led the way to the shed, leading Kate inside. Thanks to her reorganization, it didn't take him long to find what he was looking for. Kate was actually a little proud of that.

"There aren't just swords and daggers and axes," he said, lifting blade blanks and a couple of wooden blades that obviously served as models. "A rapier isn't a broadsword. An offhand blade catcher isn't a stiletto. You need to learn the differences in their balance and their weight, the way they're meant to be used and the places where they're meant to be strong."

"I want to learn all of that," Kate assured him. She wanted nothing more than that.

Thomas nodded. "I know. That's why I want you to spend the rest of the day trying blades and carving one that you think would fit you best. When you've done that, we'll work out what you've done right and what still needs work."

"Why carve it?" Kate asked. "Why not just forge it?"

Thomas looked at her expectantly. "You already know the answer to that, Kate."

"Because wood moves easier than steel," Kate said.

"Exactly." He handed her a whittling knife. "Now, get to it, and we'll see what you come up with. If it's good enough, I'll even let you forge it."

That prospect excited Kate more than the rest of it put together. She would do a good job with this. She couldn't remember her father, but right then, Thomas almost felt like one to her.

She was going to make him proud of her.

***

Kate spent the rest of the day learning that wood didn't move quite as easily as she'd thought it did. It certainly didn't move in the same way that steel did, and the skills she'd been learning from Thomas weren't of much use when it came to carving her wooden weapon.

Wood didn't flow like water when you heated it. Wood didn't bend the same way. It didn't stretch into new shapes. All you could do with it was shave from it, taking off more material to see what was left behind. That took some getting used to, and Kate found herself considering each stroke of the knife as she sought to construct a weapon that was perfect for her.

In the corner of the yard, her stolen horse whickered. To Kate, it sounded far too much like amusement.

"It's easy for you," she said. "Nobody has ever made you design a sword."

It needed to be slender and light, of course, because she wasn't as large or as strong as a boy would have been. But it still needed to have strength down toward the hilt, so that Kate could parry with it without it snapping. It would need a hilt that would protect her hand, while still being light enough to keep the balance correct. It couldn't be too short, because Kate didn't want to fight taller opponents with the added disadvantage of a blade shorter than theirs.

She whittled and she considered, shaping and reshaping, until finally, she had a blade that she thought might be good enough. It reminded her of a rapier more than the other kinds of blades, but just with the most delicate of curves to it to allow it slash

86

effectively. It was the kind of weapon that might have resulted if a saber had been designed for fighting duels, rather than hacking from horseback.

Kate lifted it, and the grip felt right in her hand now, shaped perfectly for her fingers. The weight of the sword was exactly what she'd hoped it would be, light enough that it flowed as easily as breathing as she cut with it through the air.

She tried to imagine foes in front of her, and cut at them, practicing thrusts and slices, parries and binds. In her mind, she battled the boys from the orphanage and foes from a dozen lands. She struck out and leapt back, guarding against imaginary blows.

Kate could feel the need for revenge rising in her then. She found herself picturing all the people she wanted to strike down with that sword, from the boys who'd attacked her to the masked nuns who had kept her and the others virtual prisoners. Given the chance, she would hack them all down, one by one.

In the middle of it all, she found herself daydreaming about a different time. About her sister lifting her and running through a house where there were enemies she hadn't understood. Kate had a glimpse of flames...

She stumbled, tripping on the grass of the forge's small front yard.

"Are you all right?" a voice called out, and Kate sprang up, embarrassed, looking around with hostility at the thought that someone might have seen her fall. Almost on instinct, her wooden sword came up, leveled at the newcomer.

"I'm quite glad that isn't a real blade," he said.

He was taller than Kate, with blond hair cut short in a style that suggested it was to keep it out of the way. He couldn't have been much older than Kate was, his body just starting to fill out with the muscle it would have when he was older. For now, he was slender, with a sense of wiry sense to him that Kate liked.

He was wearing the uniform of one of the mercenary companies, with a gray surcoat that had obviously been patched after some bout of fighting. Kate wasn't sure whether to be worried by that or not.

She wasn't sure what to feel about him at all, because right then her heart seemed to be trying to feel about a dozen different things at once. For what had to be the first time in her life, Kate felt herself feeling nervous around a boy.

"You don't *look* as though you're here to rob my father," the boy said.

"I'm not," Kate said. "That is... I mean... I'm Kate."

What was wrong with her? This was closer to the way Kate expected her sister to react around a handsome boy. And just the fact that she was thinking that this boy was handsome said all kinds of things that Kate wasn't sure she was equipped to think about.

The nuns in the House of the Unclaimed hadn't even tried to teach their charges about love, or marriage, or anything to do with it. The assumption had been that if the girls there ended up with a man, it would be because they'd been bought for it, and nothing more.

"I'm Will," he said, holding out a hand for her to take. Kate just about managed not to drop her wooden sword while she did it.

"I thought that you'd joined one of the mercenary companies," Kate said. "I mean, obviously you have. You're wearing a uniform."

How had she turned into something so foolish? Kate didn't know, and she didn't like it. She could see this boy's thoughts, though, and they weren't helping.

I like her. She's kind of... spiky.

"I have joined," Will said, "but we're back training and looking for more recruits. The wars over the water are getting more serious. It's good to meet you, Kate. Are you helping my father out?"

She nodded. "He's letting me stay here while I help with the forge. I'm learning from him."

She saw Will smile at that.

"That's good to hear," he said. "I was worried when I joined up. I thought he wouldn't be able to do it all. I should go in now, but... I'm glad you're here, Kate."

"I'm glad you're here too," Kate said, and then cursed herself for saying it. Who said things like that? Thankfully, Will was already heading for the house. Kate watched him go, trying not to admit to herself quite how much she enjoyed doing it, or what she felt about him then.

She liked him.

CHAPTER FIFTEEN

Judging by the light, it was later than Sophia had intended when she woke, and it took her a moment to remember that she wasn't on the streets, or in the hard beds of the House of the Unclaimed.

The sight of Sebastian beside her reminded Sophia of exactly where she was, and for a moment she tensed at the scale of the deception she'd undertaken last night. If she had any sense, she would creep away and not come back.

The trouble was that she didn't want to. Right then, Sophia felt better than she had at any point in her life. The night before had been everything she could have hoped, and more. It had been sweet, it had been passionate. It had been loving, and that part at least had caused Sophia more than a little surprise.

On instinct, she reached out to brush Sebastian's cheek with her fingers, just enjoying the sensation of him where she could touch him. Sophia felt as though she'd learned every inch of his skin the night before, but even so, she wanted to touch him again then. She wanted to be sure that he was real. That was enough to make Sebastian's eyes open, and he smiled at her.

"So it wasn't all some beautiful dream," he murmured.

Sophia kissed him for that. Well, that and the fact that she wanted to. She wanted to do a lot more than that, but Sebastian pulled back.

"Did I—" Just in time, she remembered the accent that was supposed to be hers now. "Did I do something wrong?" Sophia asked.

"No, definitely not," Sebastian assured her, and right then, Sophia could feel his thoughts as he looked at her. She expected desire, but instead, there was more than that. She could feel love. "I just need to check the time."

Sophia saw him look over to a clock in the corner of the room, its hands making it clear just how long they'd slept.

"Goddess," Sebastian said, "it's that hour already?"

The servants didn't wake me. Obviously they guessed what was happening.

Sophia caught that stray thought, and she reached out to touch his arm. "I hope I haven't made things difficult for you? I hope you don't... regret last night?"

Sebastian shook his head. "Definitely not. Don't even think it. It's just that I'm supposed to be out in the Ridings today, inspecting some of the local militias. I wish I didn't have to, but..."

"But you have duties to fulfill," Sophia said. She knew from last night how much duty was a part of Sebastian's life. "It's all right, Sebastian. I understand that you need to go."

"I hate doing these things," Sebastian said. "If it's not preparing for war, it's hunting. I keep hoping Rupert will do it all, but our mother insists."

He kissed her again before he stood to dress, and Sophia enjoyed watching him do it. She'd never thought that she would find herself like this, simply enjoying every small movement someone made, everything about them. He dressed simply today, in a dark tunic and hose worked with silver embroidery, over a shirt of pale linen. The silver buckles on his belt and shoes shone all the brighter because of it. So did his eyes.

It was a long way from what he'd worn at the ball, but it still—

"Oh," Sophia said, biting her lip. "I've just realized that all *I* have to wear is my ball gown."

Sebastian smiled at that. "I thought about that. It isn't much, but..."

He lifted a dress from a pile of clothes. It didn't have the shine and shimmer of the ball gown Sophia had stolen, but it was still more beautiful than anything she'd ever owned. It was a deep, soft green that seemed like the mossy carpet of a forest floor, and part of Sophia wanted to leap out of bed to try it on, regardless of the fact that Sebastian was still there.

She barely stopped herself in time as she remembered the mark on her calf that proclaimed what she was to the world. Perhaps the makeup from last night had held, but Sophia couldn't take the risk.

"It's all right," Sebastian said. "It's normal to feel more embarrassed by the light of day. You can try it on once I've gone."

"It's lovely, Sebastian," Sophia replied. "Far more lovely than I deserve."

It's not a tenth as lovely as she is. Goddess, is this what being in love feels like?

"You deserve far more," Sebastian said to her. He came forward to steal one last kiss from Sophia. "Feel free to go where you want in the palace. The servants won't bother you. Just... promise me that you'll still be here when I get back?"

90

"Afraid I'll turn into mist and float away?" Sophia asked.

"They say that in olden times, there were women who turned out to be spirits or illusions," Sebastian said. "You're so beautiful I could almost believe it."

Sophia watched him go, wishing all the time that he didn't have to. She stood, washed using a ewer of water, and dressed in the dress Sebastian had brought for her. There were soft brown slippers that went with it, and a light caul that went over her hair to shimmer in the sun.

Sophia slipped into it all, and then started to wonder what else she was supposed to do. On the streets, she would have gone out and started to look for something to eat. In the orphanage, they would have had chores for her to perform by now.

She set out into the outer rooms of Sebastian's suite first, seeing the spots where her clothes had fallen last night. Sophia put them away neatly, not wanting to risk losing the few things of value that she had. She found that a servant had left hard sausage, cheese, and bread in the outer chambers, so she took a few minutes to have breakfast.

After that, she looked around the rest of the suite of rooms, taking in a collection of preserved eggshells that had probably come from across the sea, and a painted map of the kingdom that looked as though it had been painted before the civil wars, because it still showed some of the free towns as independent spaces.

There was only so long that Sophia could stay in one place though. The truth was that she didn't want to just sit there alone, waiting for Sebastian to come back. She wanted to see what she could of the palace, and truly experience the life that she'd somehow talked her way into.

She stepped outside of Sebastian's apartment within the palace, half expecting someone to pounce on her the moment she did so to tell her either to leave or to return to Sebastian's rooms. Neither happened, and Sophia found herself able to wander the palace easily.

She used her talent to keep away from people, though, not wanting to risk being caught out doing the wrong thing, or being told that she didn't belong there. She avoided the spaces that had the most sets of thoughts in them, keeping to the empty rooms and corridors that seemed to stretch on for miles in the kind of tangles that could only result from hundreds of years of construction and reconstruction.

Sophia had to admit, it was beautiful there. There didn't seem to be a wall without paintings or a mural, a niche without either a statue or a decorated vase filled with flowers. The windows all had leaded panes, usually with stained glass sending different colors of light spilling across the marble floors as if an artist's paints had been overturned there.

Outside, Sophia could see gardens of breathtaking beauty, the wildness of the plant life tamed in formal rows of herbs and flowers, low trees and shrubs. She could see a formal maze out there, the bushes there higher than Sophia was tall. She started to walk with more purpose then, deciding that it would be pleasant to be able to go outside and enjoy the gardens.

The only thing that stopped her was the sight of double doors with a sign above them, proclaiming the presence of a library.

Sophia had never been in a library. The nuns of the Masked Goddess claimed that they had one, back at the orphanage, but the only books Sophia had seen them with were the *Book of Masks*, the prayer books, tracts printed by their order, and a few brief works on the subjects they claimed to teach. Somehow, Sophia suspected that this library would be very different.

She pushed at the doors more in hope than expectation, suspecting that this would be something so precious that they would lock it away from her, never allowing her anything close to access.

Instead, the oak doors swung open with well-oiled grace, letting her into a room that was everything she could have imagined and more. It stood on two levels, with one layer of shelves topped by a mezzanine level containing yet more.

Every shelf contained book after leather-bound book of all shapes and sizes, crammed together so that Sophia could barely believe that so many might exist in one place. A large table stood at the heart of the room, while nooks held chairs that looked so comfortable Sophia would gladly have curled up and slept in any one of them if she hadn't been so excited right then.

Instead of doing that, she set off around the room, pulling out books at random and checking their contents. She found books on everything from botany to architecture, history to the geography of far-flung lands. There were even books containing tales that seemed to have been entirely invented only for entertainment, like plays, but written down. Sophia had the vague feeling that the masked nuns wouldn't have approved of that.

That was probably the main reason she picked one of them, settling into one of the chairs and reading a tale of two knights who were stuck fighting one another until a long-dead lover came back from the grave to tell them which she loved the most. Sophia found herself engrossed in the words, trying to make sense of all the places it spoke about, and caught up in the idea that someone could conjure another world with nothing more than paper and ink.

Perhaps she got a little too caught up in it, because she didn't pick up the thoughts of the approaching group of girls until it was too late. When those thoughts told her exactly *who* was approaching, Sophia huddled down in her chair, hoping that the book she held would serve as enough of a shield that she wouldn't be noticed.

"I'm telling you," Milady d'Angelica said to one of her cronies, "someone drugged me last night."

"That sounds terrible," another said to her, while all the time her thoughts told Sophia that she was enjoying the other girl's predicament.

"Who could have done it?" a third asked, although *her* thoughts said that she knew exactly what her friend had intended with the prince, and she assumed it was just a mistake.

"I don't know," Angelica said, "but I do know that... *you*. What are you doing here?"

Sophia realized that the other girl was talking to her, so she stood, setting her book aside carefully.

"Was there something you wanted to say to me?" Sophia asked, taking a moment to look the other girls over. Today, Angelica still looked beautiful, in a riding outfit that said she might have been determined to catch up with Sebastian if she didn't also look a little green with the aftereffects of her poison. Of her two companions, one was shorter and plump, with medium-brown hair, while one had almost black hair falling to her waist, and was taller than Sophia.

"Why would I have anything to say to *you*?" the other girl countered, but she kept going anyway. "You took something last night that should have been mine. Do you know who I am?"

"Lady d'Angelica," Sophia answered promptly. "I'm sorry, but I don't know your first name. Still, I've heard that your friends call you Angelica anyway, so shall we stick to that?"

It was probably a foolish tone to take with her, but Sophia had seen how this girl was with anyone she considered less important. Sophia couldn't afford to back down, because that would leave her seeming weak enough to prey on. The orphanage had taught her that lesson, at least.

"You think we're *friends*?" Angelica shot back.

"I'm sure we could be good friends," Sophia answered, holding out a hand. "Sophia of Meinhalt."

Angelica ignored her proffered hand.

"A mysterious stranger who just happens to show up in time for the grand ball," Angelica said. "Claiming to be from the Merchant States. You think I wouldn't know if someone like that had been in the city? My father has interests there, and I've never heard your name."

Sophia forced herself to smile. "Perhaps you haven't been paying attention."

"Perhaps not," Angelica said, her eyes narrowing. "But I will now. You think it will take me long to learn everything about you?"

I'll write to... I don't know who I'll write to, but I'll find out.

Her thoughts didn't sound as certain as the rest of her, but even so, Sophia froze at the threat. She forced herself to think.

"And because you can't find any records in a destroyed city, you'll denounce me?" she asked. "Why, Angelica, if I'd known you would be so jealous, I would have introduced myself sooner."

"I am *not* jealous," Angelica snapped back, but Sophia could feel it rising from her thoughts like smoke. "I just want to protect Prince Sebastian from gold-digging adventuresses."

He's mine!

The strength of that made Sophia take a step back. "Well, that's very kind of you," she said. "I'll be sure to mention it to him when he gets back. I'm sure he needs protecting from the kind of person who would, for example, try to poison him to trick him into bed."

Angelica reddened at that, and even she couldn't make that look good.

"I'll find out who you are," she promised. "I'll destroy you. I'll leave you selling yourself on a street corner."

Sophia forced herself to stalk from the library, even if it was a place where she'd been planning to spend the rest of the day.

It was all she could do not to shake while she walked out.

Trouble, she sensed, was coming—and these palace walls no longer felt so safe.

CHAPTER SIXTEEN

Kate couldn't ever remember feeling as though she was a part of a family. No, that wasn't true, because she had her sister, and *that* connection was like a constant comfort at the back of her mind. She had vague images and flashes of things before the orphanage, too. A smiling face looking down at her. A room where everything had seemed much larger than a child's tiny form.

She'd never had *this* though: just sitting around a table with a family eating stew and bread, feeling as though she fit in with the rest of the people there. Thomas and Will were laughing. Even Winifred seemed happier than she'd been when Kate had arrived, but that was only to be expected. She'd come as a thief; she stayed as someone who could help around the forge.

It probably helped that Will was there too. His presence seemed to make everything better, relaxing his mother and making his father happy that he was safe. Kate just liked to watch him, and thinking that made her glance away in embarrassment.

"Are you going to be home for long?" his mother asked.

Kate saw Will shake his head.

"You know it doesn't work like that, Mother," he said. "The free companies don't sit around for long. The wars over the Knife-Water are getting worse. Havvers fell to the Disestablishers and the True Empire contingents one after another. Lord Marl's company was paid to put down an uprising in the Serralt Valley, and found that they'd formed a bandit company to rob everyone they could."

"It sounds dangerous," Winifred said, and Kate could hear the concern in her voice. Kate couldn't blame her. She wanted to protect her son.

Kate wanted to hear more about the excitement of being a soldier.

"What's it like, being part of one of the companies?" Kate asked. "Is it different from being a regular soldier?"

Will shrugged.

"It's not so different. There are only so many ways an army can work," Will said. He sounded a little like he was trying to convince himself. "Although the kingdom's standing army isn't that large anyway. It has always just relied on the loyalty of the company commanders, and the ability to buy their services."

That didn't sound like too good an arrangement to Kate.

"What happens if someone offers more?" she asked.

Thomas answered that one. "Then you get half your army switching sides in the middle of a conflict, but the dowager's ancestors were always able to outbid their enemies, and it's better than what happened in the civil wars."

"With a big central army slaughtering the people," Will said. "I don't think that the Assembly of Nobles would allow that anymore, although Prince Rupert has built up the army a little."

Kate saw Winifred shake her head.

"Enough talk about wars, and violence, and killing," she said. "It doesn't make me feel safe to know that soon you're going to be going back out to all that cruelty, Will."

"It's safe enough, Mother," he said, reaching out to take her hand. "Most of war is waiting around. The companies avoid one another where they can, and Lord Cranston is always cautious about where he commits his men."

Kate wasn't entirely happy about that. "I was hoping for tales of adventure."

"I'm not sure if I have many of those," Will replied. He obviously saw her face fall. "But I have a few. I'll tell you them some time when Mother isn't going to be worried by them."

"I worry every time you go off to fight," Winifred said.

They kept eating, and all Kate wanted to do was find excuses to ask Will more about his life. Strangely, he seemed just as interested in her.

"So, you've only been helping my father around the forge for a day?" he asked.

Kate nodded. "I... showed up last night."

"She's a thief," Winifred corrected. "Was going to rob us of everything we had."

Kate sat very still as the other woman said that. She could see that Will's mother still didn't entirely like her, and she guessed that it had a lot to do with the way she'd shown up at the forge. She couldn't help feeling, though, that it might have something to do with other things: with the talent she had, and with the mark of the indentured on her calf.

"Not everything," Thomas said, obviously picking up on Kate's discomfort. "And she's been a hard worker since, Winifred."

"Yes, I suppose so."

Kate could see enough of the woman's thoughts to know that it wasn't dislike so much as mistrust. She wasn't sure what Kate was going to do next, and it didn't help that Winifred didn't trust those with her gifts as much as her husband did. Kate pulled back, not wanting to pry where she wasn't wanted.

"This sounds like too interesting a story to ignore," Will said. "Kate, you're going to have to tell me more of it. Maybe… we could go into the city later, together?"

Even without pushing at Winifred's thoughts, Kate could pick up her shock at that.

"Will, I don't think that's—"

"I'm sure it will be fine," Thomas said. "The two of you should go out together."

Right then, there was nothing that Kate wanted more.

***

Of course, it wasn't as simple as just leaving the forge behind. Kate still had to show Thomas her work on the sword, making small adjustments as he suggested that the tang would need to be thicker with metal, and the taper on the edge less square.

Then there were the chores that Winifred suddenly found for her, from cleaning up in the courtyard to peeling vegetables in the house. It seemed obvious to Kate what she was trying to do: trying to take up so much time that she wouldn't be able to go off into the city with her son.

Kate got around it by slipping off when she wasn't watching, although Thomas was. He nodded in what seemed like permission. That was good, because Kate didn't want to risk upsetting him.

Will was waiting for her in the courtyard, and Kate could see the excitement written in every line of him there.

"Are you ready to go?" he asked. "Did you want to wash up first, or—"

"Why?" Kate countered. "Do I not look good enough to go out with you like this?"

"You look wonderful," Will said, and that was strange in itself, because Kate wasn't used to compliments. Sophia was the one people complimented, not her.

"Good," she said. "Besides, I think your mother will try to keep me here forever if we don't go now."

"Then we'd better go," Will said, with a laugh and a look back toward the house. He reached out for Kate's hand, and to Kate's own surprise, she let him take it.

They walked down toward the city, and it was clear that Will knew the way expertly, in a way that Kate didn't. He led the way down broad streets as the sun started to fall, and Kate found herself watching all the people who thronged through the streets as they walked. Most of them were just people on their way back to their homes, but there were street entertainers too: a man walking on stilts higher than Kate's head; a pair of wrestlers who fought to throw one another in a sand-filled pit.

"Where are we going?" Kate asked.

"I thought we might go down to one of the theaters," Will said. "The Old King's Players are performing a version of *The Tale of Cressa.*"

Kate didn't want to admit that she hadn't heard of either the play or the players, because she assumed that it was something *everyone* who hadn't been brought up in the House of the Unclaimed would know. Instead, she went along with Will as he led the way to a large, round, barn-like building painted on the outside with gaudy scenes. Already, there were people gathering there, waiting to be let in by the players, who stood at the door to collect a penny entrance fee.

Will paid it for both of them, and Kate found herself in the middle of a crowd so tightly packed that she could barely breathe.

"Are you all right?" Will asked.

Kate nodded. "I've just never been to a playhouse before. It's very crowded."

It wasn't long before the play began, and Kate found herself lost in the story of a girl from one end of the Curl peninsula who had to travel it in search of a boy whose love she had lost. Kate couldn't imagine going all that way for a boy, but she found herself engrossed in the spectacle of it. The Old King's Players had obviously worked out that their audiences wanted action and music, flashes of fireworks and sudden appearances. They played up to it, even if they paused here and there for speeches set to rhyme that seemed to go on longer, as if added as an attempt to make the whole thing more. Kate found herself laughing out loud at some of the comic moments, and looking on eagerly during the stage fights.

She also found her hand keeping hold of William's throughout it all, not wanting to let go of him or risk losing that contact. She didn't know about traveling the length of the Curl for him, but she would certainly fight her way through a crowded theater if she lost him.

By the time they spilled out onto the street with the rest of the crowd, Kate felt breathless with the play. She felt alive, and awake.

"We should probably head home," Will said, although his thoughts didn't agree with that.

I don't want to yet.

"In a while," Kate said, echoing his thoughts. "For now… can we just walk a while?"

Will seemed surprised by that, as if he'd been expecting her to want to go back as quickly as possible, but he nodded enthusiastically. He started to lead the way.

"Definitely. We can go up along the garden row."

Kate didn't know what that was, and found herself pleasantly surprised when Will led the way along a couple of streets to a ladder, leading up toward the roofs of the city. For a moment, Kate found herself thinking about the hiding spot that she and her sister had found, tucked in behind the chimney stacks where no one could find them to hurt them.

"You want to go up there?" Kate asked.

"Trust me," Will said.

To her surprise, Kate did, and ordinarily, she wouldn't have trusted anyone that easily. She started to climb, and it was only as they reached the top that she saw what was there. A string of trees sat impossibly at roof level, in a garden that seemed to stretch across several different houses.

"This is beautiful," Kate said. "It's like a piece of the countryside in the middle of the city."

It was more than that; it was something hopeful and defiant, standing against the overwhelming pressure of the city in a single act of growth and greenery.

Will nodded. "They say that some nobleman planted it as a place to think, but after he died, people just kept it going." They started to walk around the small number of trees, where hanging lanterns attracted lunar moths. "You probably didn't get to see much of the city, growing up in an orphanage."

Kate froze for a moment, because she knew that she hadn't told Will about that. Maybe his mother had told him, hoping to persuade him not to do this. She knew that Winifred didn't hate her exactly. She was just worried about the impact that Kate's presence might have.

"No. The door was left open, but that was like a taunt. You could leave, but you always knew that there was nowhere for you to go. And if you left and came back…"

Kate didn't want to think about some of the punishments she'd seen for that. The House of the Unclaimed had been bad at the best of times, but those had been things to leave girls broken and staring.

"It sounds awful," Will said. Kate didn't want sympathy, because she didn't want to be someone who needed it. Even so, it seemed different, coming from Will rather than from someone else.

"It was," Kate agreed. "They knew that they would be indenturing us, so they spent our lives trying to make us into obedient little things who would have just enough skills to fetch a noble's wine or work as an apprentice." Kate paused, putting her hand against a tree. "It doesn't matter, though. I'm not there now."

"You're not," Will said. "And I'm glad you're here."

Kate smiled at that. "What about you?" she asked. "I'm guessing that war isn't as boring and safe as you want to pretend to your mother."

In fact, she suspected that it was anything but safe. She wanted to hear the truth of it, the battles and the smaller engagements, the places Will had been. She wanted to hear anything he had to tell her.

"Not really," Will said with a sigh. "Lord Cranston mostly does keep us out of engagements, but when you do have to fight, it's terrifying. There's just violence everywhere. And even when you don't, there's the terrible food, the risk of disease…"

"You're making it sound so heroic," Kate said with a laugh.

Will shook his head. "It isn't. If the wars spill over the Knife-Water to here, people will find that out."

Kate hoped that wouldn't happen, but at the same time, a part of her longed for it, because it would be a chance to fight. She wanted to fight then. She would fight the whole world if she needed to. The horror of it didn't matter. There would be glory too.

"Half the time, the battles are just revenge for other battles a lifetime or more ago," Will said. "Vengeance is pointless."

Kate wasn't so sure about that. "There are a few people *I'd* like revenge on."

"It doesn't do any good, Kate," Will said. "You take revenge, and then they want revenge, until there's no one left at all." He paused for a moment, then laughed. "How did this turn so bleak, so quickly? We were supposed to be having a good time."

Kate reached out to touch his arm, wishing that she had the courage to do more than that. She liked Will.

"I am having a good time," she said. "And I think you sound very brave, with your regiment. I'd like to see it."

Will smiled at that. "I don't think it will be as dashing as you think."

Kate suspected that it would be everything she hoped and more.

"Even so," Kate said.

When Will nodded, she couldn't have been happier. "All right," he said. "But in the morning. They'll look more impressive by daylight."

Kate could barely wait.

CHAPTER SEVENTEEN

Sophia wandered the palace, and as she did so, it was impossible not to think about quite how lucky she'd been. She'd come from nowhere, and now... now it seemed as though this might actually be her *life* from now on. She had found the place she'd been looking for, and it was everything she could have ever hoped. The palace was beautiful.

Sophia wanted to be able to stay here. More than that, she wanted to be able to stay here with Sebastian. She found herself staring at a painting of some long dead noble while contemplating what she could do to make sure that Sebastian didn't ask her to leave. It was obvious that he liked her, but how did Sophia know that he was serious? She was happy in that moment, but it felt eggshell fragile. She didn't want anything to ruin it.

Sophia kept wandering, not knowing quite where to go next. She didn't want to simply go back to Sebastian's rooms, because that would feel as though Angelica and her cronies had driven her there to hide, or like she was stuck simply waiting for Sebastian to save her. She didn't want to go back to the library, because there was too much of a chance that they might be there.

Instead, she wandered up to a gallery where people walked around looking at the paintings, and then she went down toward the servants' quarters in an attempt to get the layout of the place. She went to a glass-topped solarium, where delicate plants were set to grow in the greater heat, and spent some time sitting in a nook where it seemed that no one was about to pass.

It was at that point that Sophia told herself that she was being stupid. She had at least one friend in the palace, after all.

It took her a little time to find Cora, working her way out from the ballroom until she found the space where the servant plied her trade with makeup and perfumes.

"My lady," Cora said with a smile as Sophia approached. "Come and sit down. I'll put some powder on your cheeks."

"Cora, you don't need to call me that," Sophia said.

Cora nodded. "I do, and you need to get used to it. From what I hear of things between you and Prince Sebastian, you're going to be here awhile. You need to remember who you are."

"Who I'm pretending to be, you mean?" Sophia said. Sophia of Meinhalt felt like as much of a mask as the one she'd worn to the ball.

Cora pushed her down into the chair. "You can't ever say that here. You don't know who might be listening in. From now on, you *are* Sophia of Meinhalt."

What would happen to us if the dowager found out her son had been tricked, I don't know.

Sophia caught that thought clearly. She supposed that she could understand the idea that there might be spies, or just servants in a position to hear more than they should. After all, she spent her life overhearing more than she should of people's thoughts. She could understand the danger, too. No one liked being made a fool of, and the dowager would act to protect her son, wouldn't she?

"All right," Sophia said. "But I can still come and see you, can't I? Even a noble lady needs her makeup done."

"She does," Cora agreed, and started to dust Sophia's features with a powder that turned her naturally pale complexion into something luminous and blemish free. "And while she's doing it, she can tell me how things were with a certain prince."

"Wonderful," Sophia said, unable to help herself. "He's... perfect, Cora."

Cora brushed her lips with just a hint of rouge. "He's not the man I suggested."

Was she angry about that? No, Sophia realized, with a glance through her new friend's thoughts, she was worried. Worried about all the things that might go wrong now that Sophia had picked a prince rather than some dull minor noble.

"It wasn't something I planned," Sophia said. She wanted Cora to understand that. She didn't want her thinking that she had simply decided to ignore her advice.

"It's just... it makes things more dangerous if this goes wrong," Cora said. "You know that there are rumors flying around the palace about you now?"

Sophia had guessed that there might be, simply from how much Angelica had heard about her. "What kind of rumors?"

"That you managed to brush aside Milady d'Angelica to take the prince's heart. That you're astonishingly beautiful and appeared from nowhere. That you've fled the wars across the water, and you have dangerous enemies there. I swear, half the servants are gossiping about how beautiful you are, or how wonderfully you dance."

Sophia shook her head at that. "I barely made it through the dancing without tripping over my feet."

That got a laugh out of the servant. "Do you think that matters? People see what they want to see."

Which was, of course, why Sophia had been able to succeed at this in the first place. The whole reason she had been able to find a place at court was because people wanted to see the mysterious girl fleeing a conflict, rather than the reality.

"It's just…" Cora began. "Be careful. There are already people trying to find out exactly who you are. I hear that Milady d'Angelica is asking questions, and she isn't the only one. The nobles hate it when they don't know everything there is to know."

Sophia could understand that. "I'll try to be careful."

She left, and she suspected that she looked even better than she had done for the ball. It was hard to believe that she was getting to walk around the palace with nobody challenging her. Perhaps it due to her amazement at that fact that she wasn't paying as much attention to the thoughts around her as she should have been, or perhaps she'd just gotten used to the idea that no one would bother her as she walked past them.

Either way, she turned a corner and froze as she found herself face to face with Rupert, the kingdom's heir and Sebastian's older brother.

He wasn't dressed quite as brightly as he had been for the party, but it was close. There was a *lot* of gold brocade on an outfit of red velvet, shot through with flashes of creamy silk. Like Sebastian, he was a handsome young man, although there was a confidence, even arrogance, to his demeanor that said Prince Rupert was completely aware of it. Sophia watched his eyes rove over her in a combination of surprise, amusement, and… admiration.

"Your Highness," Sophia said, with a hurried curtsey. She had to remember the etiquette, even though she could see exactly what Rupert was.

"And you are Sophia, aren't you?" He didn't bother using the lie that was her surname. With anyone else, Sophia might have taken it for friendliness. With him, she could see it was simply that he didn't feel the need to afford anyone even that much respect. She was just one more girl among a host of them, even if she was with his brother.

"Yes, Your Highness," Sophia said. "Sophia of Meinhalt."

He took her hand, drawing her up out of her curtsey with all the grace Sophia might have expected from a crown prince. He didn't let go of her hand, though, holding onto it in a way that must have seemed courtly and romantic to anyone watching, but which actually felt to Sophia as though he was holding her in place, laying claim to her as surely as a man grabbing the arm of a thief.

"I saw you at the ball last night," he said. "Dancing with my brother. You should have come over to me. We could have danced."

One glance at his thoughts told Sophia that dancing wasn't anywhere on his mind.

"You seemed busy with other partners," Sophia said with a delicate laugh.

Rupert looked her straight in the eye. "I'm not busy now, and I'd like to find out exactly what captivated Sebastian so much. Perhaps we could go somewhere."

Sophia didn't have to ask what he intended once they got there. She could see it in his mind as clearly as if someone had painted it. She found herself grateful for the powder Cora had applied to her features, because it hid the depth of her blush.

"Your Highness, I couldn't possibly. Your brother—"

"Isn't here," Rupert pointed out.

She's just a whore. Why should it matter to her?

"Your Highness," Sophia began, trying to think of a way to get out of there without having to slap the heir to the throne. She could see the way Prince Rupert saw her: as something to use because his brother had. As a prize to be claimed simply because he was the eldest. He found her beautiful, but Sophia doubted that he even saw her as a real person.

"I'm sure you found my brother sweet and gentle," Rupert said. Again, Sophia caught images that made her want to pull away. "And boring. I think you and I will not be boring when we are—"

"Sophia?"

Sophia had never been as grateful for anything as she was for the sound of Sebastian's voice right then. She managed to pull free of Rupert's grip as he came around the corner, and hurried to him.

"Sebastian," she said with all the happiness that came from not being in Rupert's grip any longer added to the normal happiness of seeing Sebastian. "You're back! I hope the day was a good one?"

"If I know my brother," Rupert said, as though nothing had just happened, "he'll have been bored out of his mind by it all. Sebastian, Mother wants us to dine with her in an hour or so. Bring Sophia. I'm sure Mother will love her. She seems delightful."

Sophia got one last flash of the things he was thinking about her before he left. It was enough to make her cling to Sebastian's arm and wish that she could wipe the things she'd seen from her mind.

"I'm glad you're here," Sophia said, leaning against him.

"I hope Rupert wasn't too overwhelming," Sebastian replied. Sophia caught the worry there. There had been girls before Sophia whom Rupert had pulled away from Sebastian when they'd realized that he was the one willing to be more extravagant. That they weren't here now only said how quickly he'd cast them aside.

"No, it's fine."

A part of her wanted to tell Sebastian exactly what had happened, but what could she say? That she'd read Rupert's mind and knew what he wanted?

"We still have some time before dinner," Sebastian said. "Would you like to take a walk around the maze for a while?"

Sophia nodded. Anything, so long as it was out of there, and with Sebastian. She walked with him out into the gardens, where lamps were starting to light up flowers that had opened in the dark, pale and silvery.

"They're midnight orchids," Sebastian said, obviously noting Sophia's gaze. "They open to attract the moths that aren't out in the daylight, so that they don't have to fight for butterflies' attention with the other flowers."

"They feel that they can't attract the butterflies?" Sophia asked. "But they're beautiful."

Sebastian touched her arm, and the contact was enough to send a shiver along Sophia's skin. "Sometimes, the most beautiful things can come along at unexpected times."

They kept going into the maze. Sophia got the feeling that Sebastian knew his way around it, because he took the turnings with confidence even though she couldn't make sense of them.

"It seems like a good place to get lost for a while," Sophia said. "Is that why you like to come here?"

"It's part of it," Sebastian said. "Although it also means we have some privacy."

Sophia made the most of it, leaning in to kiss him. She couldn't believe that she was free to do that with someone like Sebastian. That, and almost anything else she wanted. More than that, she couldn't believe that she'd found someone like him at all.

She had, though, and Sophia held close to him as they kept going through the maze.

"There's a sundial at the center," Sebastian said. "And a pergola with a chaise inside."

"I like the sound of that," Sophia said with a smile. A place for them to sit together. Potentially a place for them to do more than just sit. Sophia hadn't felt this way with anyone before. "Just so long as you know the way."

"I do."

They kept going along the close-walled stretches of the formal maze. It was comforting to know that he knew the way out of there, but even so, she found herself caught up in memories: of running along narrow corridors, running, hiding, hoping that they wouldn't be found. Of flames, licking at the edges of things so that she could feel the heat and taste the bitterness of the smoke. Telling her sister to stay quiet, because the least sound could—

"Sophia?" Sebastian said in a gentle tone.

Sophia came back to herself, looking over at him and putting her arms around him. "Sorry. I wasn't there for a moment."

"Are you all right?" Sebastian asked. "If you aren't well, maybe I can persuade my mother that it's okay for you not to come to dinner."

Sophia could see that wasn't really an option though. What the dowager wanted, it seemed, the dowager got.

"No, it's all right," she said. "I wouldn't want to make things difficult with your mother."

And yet, she had a sinking feeling that things with his mother were about to get very difficult indeed.

***

Sophia stood with Sebastian outside the doors to a small dining room, waiting for a servant to announce them. She tried as hard as she could not to let her nerves show, but the trembling of her hand in his must have given it away.

"It's all right," Sebastian said. "My mother isn't a monster."

That was easier for him to say than for her to believe. The dowager had ruled the kingdom singlehandedly since her husband's death, managing not to be overwhelmed by the Assembly of Nobles or the Church of the Masked Goddess. She'd stood through plots and economic troubles, wars overseas and threats of rebellion in the Near Colonies. Faced with her, Sophia felt certain that her deception would be unmasked in an instant.

"Prince Sebastian and Sophia of Meinhalt!" a servant announced, opening the door to a dining chamber that seemed quite small by the standards of the palace. That was to say that it was smaller than an entire building elsewhere.

There was a table there, and there were perhaps half a dozen other people seated around it, all dressed in a kind of court finery that was nevertheless a step less formal than it might have been for an official banquet. Sophia recognized Prince Rupert, but none of the others.

She quickly found herself caught in a bewildering round of introductions, obviously designed to put her at her ease, but which mostly seemed to impress on her just how out of her depth she was.

A woman in a silver gray veil was revealed as Justina, the Highest Priestess of the Masked Goddess. A man with mutton chop sideburns and graying hair turned out to be an admiral. The others were a baronet, a Shire governor, and the governor's wife. There seemed to be no particular reason for this collection of guests other than it being what the dowager wanted. Perhaps these were friends from her youth, or people in her favor who happened to be visiting.

The only thing that made Sophia more nervous was when the dowager herself walked in. Dowager Queen Mary of the House of Flamberg was not a tall woman, and age had left her gray in both hair and pallor, but there was an iron hardness to her posture that said nothing would shake her. She wore mourning black, as she had since her husband's death. She stood at the head of the table, gesturing to the others there.

"Please be seated," she said.

Sophia did so, hoping that the presence of the others might allow her to hide a little, just one more guest among all the others there. Yet, as the servants started to bring pigeon and grouse, Sophia felt those steely eyes upon her.

"Sebastian, you must introduce me to your guest, dear."

"Certainly, Mother. This is Sophia of Meinhalt. Sophia, this is my mother, Mary of Flamberg."

"Your Majesty," Sophia managed, bobbing in place as best she could.

"Ah, Meinhalt," the Dowager said. "Such a sad affair. Tell me, girl, what is your opinion of the wars that beset the continent?"

Sophia could see enough of her thoughts to know that this was a test, but not enough to know what the answer ought to be. In the end, she grabbed her answer from Sebastian's thoughts, hoping that he would know his mother well enough for it to be a good choice.

"My worry is that they won't stay there," Sophia said.

"A concern I'm sure we all share," the dowager replied. Sophia couldn't tell if she'd passed the older woman's test or not. "Although it seems that my son is grateful that at least *some* things have come over the Knife-Water. You must tell us about yourself."

Sophia did her best, trying to disguise lack of knowledge as modesty or reticence. "I came over before the city fell, Your Majesty. I think I was quite lucky in that."

"The Goddess gives her gifts," the High Priestess murmured.

"Indeed," the dowager said. "Although I seem to recall you saying that she gives us hard gifts as well as pleasant ones sometimes, Justina."

More questions followed. Had she enjoyed skating on the river in winter there? What did she think of the different sides of the war? Sophia did her best, but there was only so much her talent could help her, and only so much she knew about Meinhalt. She should have spent more time reading about it in the library. In the end, she did the only thing she could, and sought for a distraction.

"Admiral, I've always wanted to know what it's like to try to keep track of an entire navy's movements. How do you manage it all?"

"Maps, my dear," he said. "Mostly maps."

He clearly intended it as a joke, so Sophia laughed along with him. He started to go off into a discussion of the various methods of combining nautical charts. Prince Rupert interrupted, claiming that no one could possibly want to know about that, and started to talk about hunting instead. Sophia didn't mind, so long as she could keep the discussion away from her.

The eyes of the others weren't on her, for the most part, but there were exceptions. The High Priestess glanced at her from time to time with an odd look Sophia didn't dare try to read her to interpret. Sebastian seemed to be looking at her whenever Sophia looked over at him, his expression soft with love, or hopeful, or wanting to make sure that she was all right. Rupert glanced at her more than once with a hungry look that said what had happened earlier between them wasn't done. That was enough to make Sophia want to cling close to Sebastian and not let him go.

And the dowager considered her evenly, as if trying to make sense of Sophia or stare into her heart. There was something unchanging, certainly unblinking, about that gaze. That worried her more than the rest of it put together. She felt like a specimen kept under glass for examination, unable to keep anything hidden. Right then, she felt as though she was an imposter, and every glance, every word out of place, only made her feel it more. How long could she keep up this deception?

Somehow, she managed to make it through the dinner, exchanging polite conversation with the others while they ate what seemed like an entire feast's worth of food. Sophia ate sparingly, and when the time came to leave, she was only too grateful to be allowed to stand, ready to go.

Of course, there were still goodbyes to be said, and one by one, Sophia found herself taking the hands of the other guests, murmuring farewells and comments about how much she had enjoyed the evening. Even Rupert's touch didn't linger more than a second or so longer than it should have.

The dowager smiled as Sophia offered a curtsey, taking her hand instead.

"It is good to see that my son has found such a pleasant, intelligent girl to spend time with," she said, and Sophia would have been happy with the compliment in any other circumstances. As it was, she had to force herself to smile back and murmur what an honor it was, because of the thoughts she could sense behind the words.

I will find out who this girl is. A match for my son must be suitable, and girls do not appear from thin air.

Sophia had to fight the urge to run from the room. She was grateful when Sebastian took her arm, leading her from it.

"That went better than I expected," Sebastian said as they left. "I think my mother likes you."

Sophia smiled back. "I hope so."

She hoped it, but she didn't believe it. She could feel her plans unraveling beneath her, pulling apart under the weight of the dowager's suspicion. Right then, a part of Sophia wanted nothing more than to run and not come back.

No. She couldn't just walk away from all this. Not now, not after everything she'd been through, after she'd worked so hard to get to this point, taken so many risks.

And after she fell in love with Sebastian.

As much as she wanted to, she couldn't just run.

Then she realized in a flash what she needed to do: she needed to speak to her sister. Kate was the practical one. Kate would have a plan, and probably an entire way out of this mess.

She would venture out into the city streets, and do whatever she had to do to find her.

Kate, she sent. *I'm coming.*

CHAPTER EIGHTEEN

Kate could feel the excitement building in her as she walked with Will toward the outskirts of Ashton. There, the houses gave way to more open spaces, and Kate could see the greenery of the Ridings beyond, flat and open and free.

One day, she would head out into that open space, but not this morning. This morning, Kate was more interested in the spot on the edge of the city where the gray and blue flags of Will's regiment sat.

"Are you sure that you want to go see my company?" Will asked. He seemed surprised by the thought that Kate would find any of it interesting. "There are a hundred other things we could do today."

Kate caught glimpses of them in his thoughts. They could go to the theater or walk in one of the green spaces near the city. They could go and find food together in one of the taverns or wander up to a space where Will knew a fiddler would be playing and people would be dancing. All of that sounded good, but it wasn't what Kate wanted.

"I want to see what it's like," Kate said. "How am I supposed to make the best weapons if I don't know anything about the kind of people who are going to be using them?"

It was a good argument, but it wasn't the whole truth. The truth was that there was just something about the thought of one of the free companies being there that made Kate tingle with curiosity. These were men who got to travel the world, fighting enemies and visiting exotic places. She wanted to know all about it. She wanted to see it for herself.

Even so, Will seemed a bit nervous as they got closer, and Kate could see that he was worried about what might happen when he got there, and how the other members of his regiment might react to Kate. Kate was determined not to let that affect her. She wanted this.

They finally reached the space where the regiment was camped, tents spread out in a neat square for those members of it who didn't have families in the city to take them in, or who couldn't be trusted to come back if they left. Kate guessed that a part of it was also to keep the soldiers on the edge of the city where they couldn't do much damage, too.

There were men there, training and working, sitting around in the heat of the day or gambling among themselves. Kate saw raw recruits without so much as uniforms working on staying in formation while a sergeant yelled orders at them. There were more experienced men working on sword fighting and archery, musket drills and wrestling.

There was an edge to it, as well. Kate found herself picking up on concerns about the possibility of war, men training harder because they wanted to be ready in case violence came. Two men sparring with blunted steels seemed to be leaving bruises on one another with the violence of their efforts.

"I know it's not much," Will said, "and it's all a bit rough at the moment, but—"

"It's perfect," Kate said.

She started to walk the camp, gravitating to the supply tent where swords and pikes, crossbows and blunderbusses stood in neat stacks. Molds for shot stood next to sharpening stones for knives and halberds. A shaven-headed quartermaster looked at her with suspicion until he saw that Will was with her, then let her move among the weapons, admiring the work.

"Looking for flaws in the blades?" he asked, although it was obvious that he didn't believe Kate would have a clue where to start.

"Well, the edges on those knives could use some work," Kate said, "and I think that axe has picked up some warps in the edge while it was hardening."

Now the quartermaster looked at her with a level of surprise that Kate found a little insulting.

"Kate has been learning from my father while I've been gone," Will said.

"Why shouldn't I know about swords?" Kate demanded.

She kept walking around the camp, taking in everything that was going on there, from the eagerness of the recruits as they worked to learn the skills of soldiering to the careful, energy-saving movements of the veterans.

In that moment, Kate knew that this was even closer to what she wanted than life at the forge was. In the forge, she was getting to make weapons and learn about them, but these men got to use them. They had lives where they traveled and fought, worked together and got away from the mundanity of the city.

112

More than that, if there was any path that might let Kate move closer to vengeance, this was the one.

"Would you like to spar?" Kate asked Will, picking up two of the wooden practice blades. They were heavier than the one she'd designed, the oak handles rough in her hand.

"Are you sure?" he asked.

In answer, Kate tossed one to him. Will caught it, bringing it up into a guard position. Kate copied him. He struck at her slowly, and she deflected it, thrusting back at him. They went back and forth, and Kate felt as though she was catching the rhythm of it, deflecting those blows that came too close to her, while swinging her own strokes back for Will to parry. The swords were heavy, but Kate managed to keep hers in the way of the attacks that came toward her.

"Trying to get her ready to join the company, Will?" an older man called over. "Or just trying to impress her?"

Kate stepped back, wondering what it would be like. She and Will could go around together, fighting alongside one another, traveling to places Kate had barely heard about.

"Maybe I want to join," Kate said, putting her fists on her hips.

The veteran laughed as if that were the best joke he'd heard all day.

"You want to join? Oh, that's a good one. You should have brought her before this, Will. We can always use a good laugh."

Kate could feel her hand tightening around the hilt of her wooden sword.

"I'm serious," she snapped.

"Hear that, lads?" the veteran called out, and still, it seemed as though he was repeating a good joke he'd heard. "She's serious. She wants to join Lord Cranston's men!"

That got more laughs from around the camp, and now a rough circle of men started to form around Kate and Will. They'd obviously decided that there was entertainment to be had here.

Kate could sense just how worried Will was by all of it. He wanted to walk away right then. He wanted to get Kate back to the forge before anything else could happen. Kate stood there instead, facing up to them.

"Why *shouldn't* I join you?" Kate demanded. "If you're all so worried that war might be coming, aren't you going to need everyone you can get?"

"Every *man* we can get," the veteran said. "The regiments are no place for girls. Especially not ones barely old enough to be away from their mothers."

Kate could feel her expression hardening as her anger rose. "Shut your mouth. You know nothing about my mother."

She saw the veteran shrug. "Oh, are you going to make me? Dancing around with your wooden sword as if you have a clue what you're doing with it? Will was being soft with you, girl. Do you want to know what a real fight feels like?"

Kate could feel herself getting angry now. "I know what a fight feels like."

That got another laugh from the assembled men, and there was a kind of cruelty behind it. Kate caught thoughts of battles, of moments when men had come at them with blades. They weren't taking her seriously. Even Will looked more as though he wanted to get Kate out of there than like he wanted to support her.

"I don't think you do," the veteran said. He gestured toward one of the younger recruits, a boy who had more fat than muscle, but even so was bigger than Kate. "You, get out there with a practice blade. Let's show the little girl why she isn't cut out for war."

The boy stepped forward, looking nervous as he took a wooden sword. Even so, he stood out in front of Kate, adjusting his grip as he raised his weapon, as if trying to remember what he was doing.

"This isn't a good idea," Will said. "Why don't we just—"

"You brought her here," the veteran snapped. "Now remember where you stand in this company and get out of the way. If the girl wants to fight, she can fight."

Kate reached out to put a hand on Will's shoulder. "It's all right, Will."

She stepped out to face up to her opponent, raising her weapon the way she had when training with Will. The men around her laughed, or joked to one another, or made bets on exactly how long she would last.

"The fight keeps going until one of you gives in," the veteran said. "You want to be one of us, girl? You have to show us that you're not weak. Begin!"

Her powers gave her plenty of warning of the first couple of attacks, letting her dodge back out of range so that they cut through the air. But her powers weren't a perfect guide, and Kate still had to rely on her reflexes and her reactions, parrying on instinct, trying to get her sword in the way.

When she did, the impact jarred down her arm. The recruit she was facing might have weight to lose, but he still hit with all the power that his size gave him. Kate's sword shivered with each blow, and she knew that this boy wanted to hurt her then. He wanted to prove to the men there that he was one of them; that he had the same toughness, the same ruthlessness. Kate gave way under the attacks.

Kate could see then just how much Will had been holding back when he'd been fencing with her. There hadn't been this relentless impact, or this level of aggression behind the blows. Despite it, Kate gritted her teeth and tried to fight back. She guessed that she would at least have greater speed than the boy, although the weight of the practice blade made even that difficult.

Kate cut and thrust, only to find her blows blocked with as much violence as there had been in the boy's attacks before. Kate stepped back, trying to think, working out if she could manage to feint past the boy's parries, perhaps, or slip around him with her smaller size and agility.

"Don't stand there!" the veteran yelled. "Attack her! Close her down!"

Kate wanted to complain about the boy being coached from the sidelines, but there was no time for it. The boy charged at her, pressing in, forcing his blade against hers as he pushed closer. Like that, there was no space for Kate to use her speed, while he could bring his full size and strength to bear.

He hit out with the hilt of his wooden training sword, the rounded basket of it catching Kate across the jaw. She felt the clunk of wood meeting bone with a jarring thud, and for a moment, the world seemed to spin. The boy hit her again, and she fell to one knee.

"Don't stop," the veteran called. "If a foe is down, you finish them!"

Kate tried to raise her sword to block the next blow, but the impact of it was enough to jar the weapon from her hand this time, sending it spinning into the muddy grass. The boy struck her once, then again, with the wooden blade. He didn't hold back, as if to do so would be to show weakness in front of the others. Instead, his face reddened with the effort of swinging it, as if the fact that Kate was still there was only making him angrier.

Kate had been beaten before. She knew that the art of it was to absorb the blows, to never show pain, to just accept what you couldn't change. She couldn't give in to that, though. Instead, she threw herself forward, trying to tackle the boy and keep the fight going.

The hilt of the wooden sword struck her across the jaw again and she fell full length to the grass. The boy brought the sword down across her shoulders, then her back, obviously determined not to stop until he was told.

Will was there then, wrenching the blade from his hands with ease. Kate guessed that she should have been grateful that he was stepping in, but right then, it just felt like a demonstration of how unskilled the opponent had been who had just beaten her. Will went to help her up, and Kate brushed away his help, forcing herself back to her feet.

"I can do it," she said.

"About all you can do," the veteran snapped from the sidelines. "Will, get this girl out of our camp. I don't want to see her again. The only place for women in the army is as wives and whores."

Kate wanted to spit in his face, but she suspected that would just earn her another beating, and right then, she could barely stand from the one she'd just had. This time, when Will took her arm, she let him.

"Come on," Will said, "we need to get out of here before they decide to do something worse."

Kate nodded, letting him help her from the training field. She had never felt as humiliated as she did then. She'd thought that she could fight, but one bigger boy had been enough to beat her. She would have added his name to the list of those she wanted revenge on, but that was a problem in itself.

How could she ever hope to take revenge if she couldn't even win a fight on a practice field? How could she do it when she was this weak, this helpless?

CHAPTER NINETEEN

Sophia felt strange, slipping out of the castle grounds and into the city. One of the guards on the gates fell into step with her, and she turned, staring at him, not knowing what he wanted.

The prince will have our posts if we let anything happen.

"You're following me because you think it's what Prince Sebastian wants?" Sophia asked.

"Yes, my lady," the guard said.

A part of her wanted to tell him that it wasn't what *she* wanted, because there were places she needed to go today that were better visited unobserved. She didn't, though, and not just because it would have been suspicious for a noblewoman to turn down that kind of protection.

The truth was that Ashton *was* a dangerous place. Just the thought of having to go down into it filled Sophia with a sense of fear at all the things that might happen. She'd seen the darker side of the city in her brief time on the street, and worse, she knew there might still be hunters out there.

"Very well," Sophia said, trying to think how a noble would put it, "but some of this is... a delicate matter. I can trust your discretion?"

"Absolutely, my lady. Would you like me to carry your bag?"

Sophia clutched the leather sack she'd had a servant bring closer. The contents could get her into too much trouble.

"It's fine," she said. "There is a gift for Sebastian involved." The lie came easily enough. It was the only thing Sophia could think of that might ensure the prince didn't hear every detail.

"He will not hear about it from me," the guard promised.

First, though, she had a message to send.

Kate? Can you hear me?

She didn't get an answer, of course. It was too much to ask that their power would operate as smoothly across a city as across a room. Even so, Sophia summoned up an image of one of the squares below the palace, hoping that her sister would get it and be able to come.

It was impossible to know if Kate had gotten the message, so Sophia set about her *other* task in the town. She asked around the square, being discreet, lifting thoughts where she needed to until she found what she was looking for. It was hard to do it with the presence of the guard just a few paces behind, but to his credit, he didn't comment or try to dissuade her. She could see why from his thoughts.

Nobles do strange things. It's not my place.

When she reached the pawnbroker's shop, Sophia did her best to look the part of a nervous young noblewoman. It didn't take a lot of acting, just a few thoughts about what might happen if the wrong people saw her here. It was bad enough that there was still the guard near her, watching her every move.

"Wait here for me," Sophia ordered, and then plunged into the shop.

Inside, a man in an expensive suit of clothes that had obviously been patched many times regarded her warily.

"What can I do for you... my lady?"

"It's delicate," Sophia said.

"Discretion is my watchword."

"I find myself short of funds in the wake of the latest ball, and obviously I can never wear that dress again... would you be interested in such things?"

It turned out that he was, although at nowhere near what they were truly worth. Even so, the small pile of Royals and shillings he handed over seemed like a fortune. For the first time, her theft of the clothes seemed like what it was, because now Sophia could see exactly how much she'd taken from Angelica and the others.

Still, she would need the money if she was going to play the part of the noble Sophia of Meinhalt, and she couldn't afford to keep the dress where it might one day be recognized. It was better to be safe, to get rid of it.

She had just concluded the transaction when she glanced out of the shop's window and saw a familiar figure on the edges of the crowd. Sophia saw her sister watching as though ready to run at the first hint of trouble.

Taking a guard with her to see Kate probably wouldn't be a good idea.

"Is there another way out of here?" Sophia asked.

"My lady is *very* cautious about being seen," the pawnbroker said. "You needn't worry. There's a reason why I'm so close to the noble quarter."

He let her out of a back door nonetheless, and Sophia slipped around past the spot where the guard was standing. She was able to buy two eel pies and some beer while she walked back across the square to her sister. She found herself wondering how things had gone for Kate in the last couple of days, and hoping that they had gone well. She certainly hoped that things were less complicated for her sister than they were for her.

The moment Sophia saw her sister walking toward her in the square, the moment she saw Kate's face, she knew that things were anything but simple for her.

There were bruises there, and it seemed as though she had a split lip, only just beginning to scab over. One of her hands was bandaged, as if from a burn, and she was moving without her usual energy and strength. Sophia ran to her, wrapping her arms around Kate.

"What happened to you?" Sophia asked. "Are you all right?"

"It's nothing," Kate said, and Sophia could see the look of determination there that meant that Kate was trying to be brave.

You can't hide things from me, Sophia sent, and this close, it wasn't like some blind sending across the city. *What happened?*

"All kinds of things," Kate said. She took one of the eel pies when Sophia offered it. "It's part of why I could come. Thomas let me off from the forge after everything."

"Is he the one who did this?" Sophia asked. She didn't know what she could do to someone who had hurt her sister like this, but she would find something.

"What?" Kate asked. "No! This... it's embarrassing. I tried to join one of the free companies."

"You tried to join a regiment?" Sophia said. "And they *beat* you for it? That's where all these injuries are from?"

"Not all of them," Kate admitted. "I got the burn when I was clumsy in the forge. Oh, and some barge hands threw me off a barge when I tried to leave the city."

That was the last thing Sophia wanted to hear. She wanted her sister to be *happy*.

"Oh, Kate, why couldn't you stay safe? Be the kind of girl who likes to sit in the library and read?"

"I am, remember?" Kate countered. "I took us there."

Sophia had forgotten that the library had been the first place they'd gone looking for safety. It seemed like a lifetime ago, even though it had just been a matter of days.

"You'd love the library in the palace," Sophia said. "They have more books than anyone could hope to read."

"You should love it there then," Kate said. "I can't believe that you made it inside."

"It wasn't easy," Sophia assured her. "I had to sneak into the middle of a ball."

Sophia started to tell her the story of it, and she watched her sister's eyes widen in response.

"You seduced a *prince*?" Kate said, in obvious disbelief.

"I think... we kind of seduced each other," Sophia said. She didn't want to think about what she had with Sebastian as the kind of simple manipulation some nobles perpetrated with those who had more money. "He's wonderful, Kate."

"And you're obviously doing well," Kate said, with a gesture toward Sophia's rich clothes.

"Yes, I..." Sophia hesitated, then shook her head. "It's dangerous here too. Already, there are people asking questions, wondering who I am. They might not be beating me, but there are girls there who... I upset them when Sebastian picked me. They won't forget."

Kate reached out to put a hand on her arm. "It sounds as though we should both be careful. Are you sure you're doing the right thing?"

"Are you?" Sophia countered. She couldn't let Kate see the truth: that she wasn't sure. That there was a part of her that wanted to walk away from all of it before it went too badly wrong. She had some money. She and Kate could get on a boat on the river and head out of the city. Except... she wasn't sure that she could leave Sebastian that easily.

"I need to do this," Kate said. "These bruises are nothing. I'm *going* to learn to fight. I'm *going* to get to where I don't have to rely on *anybody*."

To Sophia, she sounded like she was trying to convince herself, but Sophia didn't say anything. She knew what it was like to want to believe that things would turn out all right, even though there were so many things that could go wrong.

"And," Kate said, "there's a boy. His name is Will."

Her sister sounded hopeful now. Sophia knew that tone, because she heard it in her own voice when she spoke about Sebastian.

"Tell me about Will," Sophia said with a smile.

"He's wonderful," Kate said. "It was his regiment I was going to, and—"

"And you were trying to impress him?" Sophia asked.

Kate looked a little embarrassed. "A little."

Sophia put an arm around her sister. "Kate, you shouldn't be doing things that could get you hurt."

"Neither should you," Kate countered. "It sounds really dangerous in the palace." She paused for a moment. "We could still

120

run away. Come with me now. We could just go, leave the city and find somewhere else."

Sophia wished that she could. She wanted nothing more than to look after her sister and make sure that she never came to harm again.

"I can't," she said instead, even though it hurt to do it. "I have to do this. I have to go back."

Kate hugged her. "Are you sure?"

Sophia wasn't sure, but she couldn't let her sister see that.

"You can rely on me," she said instead. "If I hear you calling, I'll come."

"Me too," Kate promised. "Wherever you are, wherever you go, I'll come if you need me. I'll storm the palace if I have to."

She probably would, and just the thought of that made Sophia smile.

"In the meantime, take this," Sophia said, pressing most of the coins she'd gotten for the dress into her sister's hand. "And Kate? Maybe try to spend more time in libraries than getting beaten?"

She saw her sister nod.

"Maybe I will," Kate said. "Maybe I will."

***

Kate made her way back through the city, keeping her usual watch for anyone who might want to harm her. The fight down at the training grounds had taught her that there was always someone who would try to hurt her. Wherever she went, someone would want to prove that they were stronger, or that she was worthless.

She'd almost asked Sophia to help get her out of everything she was caught up in, almost asked her big sister to pluck her out of danger like some helpless child. If she hadn't been able to see how precarious things were for Sophia too, Kate might even have done it.

Or maybe not. Not before she'd learned to fight. Not before she'd had her revenge. Her sister had been able to give her a clue of how to do that, at least.

She hadn't been to the penny library since the day she and Sophia had run from the House of the Unclaimed. Even now, approaching the old structure felt like a stupid move, because what if someone was watching, waiting for her to do it? Kate could only trust that even the masked nuns wouldn't be that vindictive. They had more girls than just her to torment, after all.

She crept inside, and sure enough, Geoffrey was there on the outer desk, casting what he probably thought was a stern eye over those who tried to enter. When Kate approached, she could see his surprise.

"Kate, they didn't catch you. I... I'm glad. And I'm sorry that I didn't dare to hide you."

Kate didn't tell him that she forgave him. She wasn't in the habit of forgiving people. Even so, she waved it away, taking out a penny from the money Sophia had just given her.

"I want to use the library. Are you going to call for the watch while I do it?"

"No, of course not. And you don't need to pay. I owe you that much, at least."

He owed more than that, but for now, Kate was prepared to ignore it. There were things that she needed to know, and Geoffrey always had a good idea of where to find things in the chaotic organization of the penny library.

"Where can I find books on fighting, Geoffrey?" Kate asked. "*Are* there books on it?"

Geoffrey spread his hands. "There are. We have tales of some of the great warriors of the past, and manuals on the modern warfare with pikes and muskets. There are even a couple of books written by the sword masters of the continent."

Kate started with those, because they seemed the most promising, yet in some ways, they were the most disappointing books she had read. One contained string after string of illustrations, but they had no words to accompany them, and seemed to be in an entirely random order. Another was written in one of the languages from across the Knife-Water, and even without knowing the words, Kate could see that it was more about showing how many things the writer knew than about teaching them. It was a way to proclaim his skills, or perhaps to secure a post as a fencing master, not something designed to learn from.

She started to read the books that focused on the tales of the great warriors of the past instead: Renaud of Bevan, the islander McIlty. Kate could see from the start that they were just collections of folk tales, and even the parts that talked about how they had achieved their great strength seemed like nothing Kate could hope to do. Carrying a calf around on her shoulders every day until it was full grown? Wrestling every man she met until all kept clear of her? They sounded impossible.

The next book didn't seem much better. It was a slim, strange volume, which seemed to be half sword manual, half fantastical account of the life of a swordsman named Argent. It had seemed promising at first, because his work claimed that he came from Ashton, but there were fragments that seemed like pure fiction. There was even a section claiming that he had started life as a skillful but weak swordsman, but had gained strength by going to a woodland glade south of the city and cheating the spirits he found at a fountain there. It came complete with a map, claiming to show the spot he'd gone to and pointing to signs that led there: a way marker, a set of stone steps, and more. Kate sighed and put the book down harder than she probably should have.

"Careful, Kate," Geoffrey warned her. "You know better than to damage books others might want to read."

"I can't see anyone wanting to read this," Kate shot back. "Swordsmen who get their strength from magic fountains? Unbeatable blade masters who appear out of nowhere? It's nonsense."

She saw Geoffrey glance down at the book. "That's Argent's story, isn't it? Yes… yes, you're right… you should ignore it."

I don't want her to end up like he did. It's better if she thinks it's a fable.

"Geoffrey," Kate said, "what aren't you telling me? This Argent was a real person."

"No, I just told you…"

Real, and dangerous.

"Geoffrey," Kate said in a warning tone. "You wouldn't help me when I needed you. You owe me. Tell me the truth."

Geoffrey seemed to wilt, looking down.

"Argent was a swordsman when I was young," he said. "He wasn't very good. Then he went away from the city. Not for long. Certainly not for long enough to be as good as he was when he came back. He defeated d'Aquisto and Newman one after the other in practice bouts! When people asked him how he did it, he talked about a fountain south of the city, and that's all he would ever say about it."

"You're saying it's real?" Kate asked. "You're saying that I could—"

"No, Kate," the librarian insisted. "You couldn't. Because you know what happened to Argent? He disappeared, right at the height of his talents. He fought everyone there was to fight, he wrote his book, and then he *vanished*. There are those who say that the Masked Goddess's priests took him, but there are others… others who say that it was someone, *something*, else."

123

Kate could feel the fear coming off Geoffrey then. He was serious about this, but that seriousness didn't make her share his fear. Instead, it excited her, because it meant that it was real. This fountain might exist.

"Promise me, Kate," he said. "Promise me that you won't go to look for this. It's dangerous."

"I promise," Kate said, raising her hand as if to swear an oath. At the same time, she found herself thinking about the map she'd seen in the book, trying to remember the details of it.

It seemed to be enough for Geoffrey. Kate heard him breathe a sigh of relief and he returned to his books while Kate contemplated her next move.

It was probably as well right then that she was the one who could read the librarian's mind, and not the other way around. It meant he couldn't see what Kate really intended.

It meant he couldn't see the lie.

CHAPTER TWENTY

Sophia returned to the palace, slipping in as quietly as possible, but unable to avoid the glances of some of the people there. She saw servants hurrying off at the sight of her, and wondered who they were rushing to tell. She saw Angelica looking down from a balcony, with an expression like thunder.

Something was happening, and people were moving too fast for Sophia to lock onto any one of them to find out what. She had vague impressions of violence and tension, of men preparing for conflict, yet why would Angelica be upset about that? It made no sense.

For a moment, the uncertainty of it all was almost enough to make Sophia turn around and head back into the city, because something had to be wrong, and right then, the only thing that Sophia could think of was that they might have found out about her. If they knew, she needed to run and run now.

If that were the case, though, wouldn't Angelica look triumphant? Why wouldn't she be there to gloat as she saw Sophia brought low? That thought was enough to make Sophia keep going, into the palace, looking for answers. Looking for *Sebastian*.

She didn't have to look far to find him. He was waiting for her at the entrance to his rooms, looking surprisingly soldierly in a royal blue surcoat, a backsword hanging at his hip. He extended a gloved hand towards Sophia, and she took it.

"Sebastian? Is something happening?"

Sebastian nodded. "Lots of things. For a start, I have a day planned for us."

He smiled as he said it, not saying more. In his thoughts, Sophia caught a jumble of things. There was... a boat?

There was indeed a boat. Sebastian walked with Sophia down to a small tributary of the river that ran through the city, surrounded by the palace grounds, with kingfishers flitting down into one of the rare clear patches of water in Ashton. There was a small boat there carved with dragons and gilded until it shone, with a quartet of blue liveried men sitting at the oars, and a couch on a small deck above.

Sebastian helped her to it, and the boat glided from its moorings with smooth strokes. On the grass of the riverbank, a pair of golden pheasants strutted, while Sophia thought that she could see deer in the distance.

"It's beautiful here," Sophia said. "More beautiful than the rest of the river."

"We're fairly high upstream," Sebastian said. "Before the city has affected it too much."

Sophia guessed that Ashton could take anything and make it into something ugly. It certainly did it with people often enough, hardening them into shapes willing to take anything from others. Somehow, though, in the middle of it all, Sebastian wasn't the same. He was kind, and generous, and perfect.

They rowed down through the city to another stretch of greenery, where willows arched over the water, and a small jetty led to a garden filled with colorful blooms, which in turn attracted buzzing bees and brightly colored butterflies. There was also a blanket spread out, with a picnic laid upon it.

"You planned all this for me?" Sophia asked.

"All this and more," Sebastian assured her. He gestured to a spot where an easel was set up just beyond the picnic blanket, and a woman in an artist's smock sat by it, already working on the background of the garden scene.

"Who is that?" Sophia asked.

"That is Laurette van Klet," Sebastian said. "She's going to be a major artist, bigger than Hollenbroek, once the nobles around here see her work. I couldn't think of anyone better to paint you."

"To paint *me*?" Sophia said. Even the idea of it caught her a little by surprise. The idea that someone might want to paint her seemed like something unreal, something impossible. The paintings she'd seen in the palace had been of princes and kings, queens and noblewomen. There had been allegorical figures too, mythological scenes and women of the greatest beauty. There hadn't been any orphans that Sophia could see.

"Do not let my presence distract you," the woman said. "I have no use for the stuffy formality of others' portraits. Continue as you were."

It was a strange feeling, being ordered to enjoy herself the way a general might have ordered troops into battle. Even so, Sophia tried, lying on the picnic blanket while Sebastian moved in close beside her, offering her a quail's egg.

It was so beautiful, lying there in the sun, nibbling at sweetmeats and pastries, kissing Sebastian, just enjoying this closed off space that it seemed the rest of the world could not touch. Sophia kept close to Sebastian, and it was easy to get lost in his presence, so that despite the artist a little way away, and despite the oarsmen who had brought them there, it felt to her as if they were alone in the world.

Then the rowers brought instruments from the boat and started to play, on harp and low flute, tambour and lute. The sheer incongruity of it made Sophia laugh.

"There!" Laurette called out. "I want to capture your face like that."

To Sophia's surprise, she didn't ask Sophia to hold the posture though. She just put her fingertips to her temples, as though trying to drill the moment into her brain.

"It's her gift," Sebastian said. "She can remember a moment and paint it perfectly."

"Why would you paint it any other way?" the artist asked, sounding surprised by the very idea.

Sophia could see her looking Sophia over, from the way she lay on her side to the way her dress had ridden up her calves just a little. By the standards of the stuffy portraits she'd seen in the palace, this one would probably be revolutionary, or at least shocking.

Sophia stayed there, and it was a strange feeling now, knowing that someone was watching every move she made. What would Sebastian's mother make of the portrait? Would it make the dowager think that she was an even less likely match for her son than she must have after the dinner the other night?

"All of this," Sophia said. "I get the feeling that you're trying hard to impress me, Sebastian."

"Shouldn't I?" he countered. "I would give you the world if you let me."

It was one of those things that sounded as though it was far too romantic to be true, but Sophia could see that Sebastian meant it, exactly as he said it. He would literally give her anything; wanted to give her everything.

He seemed to have started with the finest delicacies the palace's kitchens could produce. There were slices of roasted venison on black bread, sweet tarts that contained berries from the palace gardens, topped with saffron that must have come in on a merchant ship. There was even a pie that held goose, duck, and quail, all layered within one another.

"All of this." Sophia shook her head. "It's enough that you're here with me." She was even more surprised to see that *she* meant it too. She'd come to the palace with the intention of securing a better life for herself, but right then she wouldn't have minded being in a shack, so long as Sebastian was there with her. "You don't have to go out of your way to do anything else."

"That's a sweet thing to say," Sebastian said. "But I want everything to be perfect for you."

It was perfect. Since she'd arrived at the palace, it had been as though she was walking in a dream, and not one of the dreams that plagued her at night, with half-remembered images of a house in flames, running through corridors with her sister. This had been, instead, the kind of dream that had seemed impossible in its beauty, offering things that Sophia had assumed would recede come daybreak.

Yet here she was, with a prince of the realm, eating the finest food, being serenaded by skilled musicians, having her portrait taken. If someone had told her that this would happen even a few short weeks ago, Sophia would have assumed that it was a joke, and a cruel one at that. She would have assumed that it was just a way to make her indenture worse with the promise that it might not come to that.

"Is something wrong?" Sebastian said, reaching out for her.

Sophia took his hands, kissing them both. "Just memories of the past."

"I don't want anything to be wrong today. I want at least one perfect day, before…"

Sophia cocked her head to one side. "Before what, Sebastian?"

She saw the answer to that before he said it, and she was already paling with the words she took from his mind when he told her.

"You've heard that the wars are getting worse?" Sebastian said. He shook his head. "What am I saying? You've seen for yourself how bad things have become, with all the different sides, the petty wars."

"But they aren't here," Sophia pointed out. She wished that she could do more than that. She wished that she could make all the wars, the threats, and the worries go away for Sebastian.

"Not yet," Sebastian said, "but the wars are like small streams flowing into a river, and that river is flowing toward us. When there were a dozen sides fighting one another, it was easy to ignore, and being an island helped for a while, but now, with everything here… there are those who think that we're weak."

"And so you're going to show them that you aren't," Sophia said. "Hoping that they won't strike back."

There was more bitterness in that than she intended. She'd seen what violence could do firsthand, even if she hadn't been in the

128

war. More than that, she found herself worrying about Sebastian. She didn't want to risk him being hurt.

"It's something that's necessary," Sebastian said. "More importantly, it isn't something I have a lot of choice about. Mother has decided that I need to look more like a real prince."

Sophia would have laughed at that if it hadn't been so serious. Sebastian was going off to war, where there were no guarantees of safety. Where anything could happen.

"More like Rupert, you mean? Trust me; compared to him, compared to *anyone*, you are the perfect prince."

"I wish it were just you making the decision," Sebastian said. "Then I could stay here with you. As it is, my mother says that I have to look like a prince to the Assembly of Nobles. That's why I've been given a commission. I'm to be an officer in the royal house cavalry."

"Endeavoring to be as dashing as possible?" Sophia asked, but even as she asked it, she could feel her heart falling.

More than that, she found herself feeling a building suspicion. There had been wars on the continent for as long as Sophia could remember, but it was only *now* that Sebastian's mother was sending him to take part? Was it really about some build-up in the violence, or was the dowager just looking for a way to separate her son from the girl he'd just met? Sophia knew that Sebastian's mother didn't trust her.

Or maybe Rupert had done it. Perhaps the elder brother had whispered the right things in his mother's ears about making a man of Sebastian, or the need to be seen to be doing well in the wars. Sophia had seen the jealousy when the two of them had been together. She'd also seen what he wanted from her. Was this just a way to isolate her?

Sophia didn't want to think more about what it might mean. There was the risk to Sebastian, the danger that came with a war... but also the more practical problem that he wouldn't be there. At best, she would be left in the palace waiting for him. At worst, they might ask her to leave the moment his protection was gone. They might cast her out in a way that would be a petty insult to a real noble, but which would be devastating to her.

"Don't be afraid, Sophia," Sebastian said. "I'm sure I won't be in any danger, and I won't let anything happen to you, either. That's part of why I did all this. I want to make certain."

Sophia frowned slightly. "Make certain of what?"

"That you'll say yes."

Sophia's heart was in her mouth as Sebastian stood, returning to the space where their boat was moored. There was something in his hand, and when Sophia saw the jewelry box there, she barely dared to breathe. She could think of at least one thing Sebastian could do that would explain a lot of what was happening today. Something that would also do a lot to explain how furious Angelica had looked back at the palace.

When Sebastian fell to one knee, Sophia stood in surprise, but that only made it easy for him to take her hand, holding it in one of his while he opened the box he held.

The ring inside shone white gold, with diamonds that must have come from the other side of the world, and deep purple sapphires that were almost as rare. The band was a thing of intertwining strands, plaited into something delicate and elegant. It was the kind of ring that a master jeweler had probably worked for days over, and it had a sense of age to it that suggested it had probably been a royal heirloom since well before the civil wars.

"Sophia," Sebastian said. "I had wanted to take my time before this, but the truth is that I already know what I want when it comes to you, and I… I want to do this before I have to go. I want you to be my wife."

"You're asking me to marry you?" Sophia asked.

Sebastian nodded.

There was only one answer to that. It overwhelmed any objection Sophia might have thought of, any concern she might have had about how other people might react. She pulled Sebastian up into her arms, holding him tightly as she kissed him.

"Yes, Sebastian! Yes, I'll marry you."

CHAPTER TWENTY ONE

Kate almost hit her hand three times the next day, she was so distracted. She kept looking over to the spot where her stolen horse was tethered, happily chewing on grass and old oats. The first time it happened, Thomas laughed and told her to be careful. The second time, he frowned.

This time, he stopped in the middle of forging a set of horseshoes, letting the flames dull back down to an orange glow.

"No, don't stop because of me," Kate said. "If you stop working the metal, it will—"

"I know what it will do," Thomas said. "But I'd rather waste the effort than have you break all your knuckles swinging a hammer blind."

Kate didn't want that either, but she was willing to take the risk if the alternative was letting the smith down. She wasn't going to ruin his work just because she was busy dreaming about fountains that could grant skill with a sword.

"What is it?" Thomas said. "Is Will out there to distract you?" He went over to the window. "The horse? Are you thinking of leaving us, Kate?"

There was a note of disappointment in that, and Kate could understand it. Thomas had given her so much, and here she was, not paying attention to the work that he had for her.

"It's not that," Kate said. "It's just... you heard what happened at the training ground?"

She saw Thomas nod, and guessed that he'd had the details from Will. Either that, or one of the soldiers had spoken about it when they'd come to have a dent hammered out of a greave or a helmet.

"There's a place where I could learn to fight," she said.

"You'd ride off there and not come back?" Thomas asked.

"I'd come back," Kate insisted. "I don't want to stop being here."

She was surprised to find that it was true. This was the first time that she'd had anything like a real home; the first time that she'd had people who seemed to care about her. Even Winifred seemed to in her way. It was just a way that was deeply worried for her son's and her husband's well-being. This was the first place where Kate had felt as though she was doing something useful.

Then there was Will. Kate wasn't sure what there was with Will, not yet. She'd never had a chance to see boys as anything except bullies and threats, yet now here one was and she liked him. She liked him a lot.

"Then it sounds as though you should go," Thomas said. "Before your distraction means that you hurt yourself."

"But—" Kate began. She'd been intending to finish the work for the day, at least.

Thomas shook his head. "I'll get by without an apprentice for another day. Or two, if you need it. Go on with you. I'll try to salvage these horseshoes."

Kate didn't need a second invitation. She hurried out to the horse she'd stolen, looking around until she found the tack for it and then starting to fasten it all in place. She was halfway through it when she saw Will coming out of the house.

"Kate? You're not going, are you?"

He sounded worried that she might be, maybe worried that she would want to leave after what had happened with his regiment.

"I'm not leaving forever," Kate said, and smiled at the thought that it was the kind of thing a boy might say when he was going off to war. "It's just… there are things I need to do. I need to get stronger."

"Why?" Will asked. "You're safe here. I could protect you."

Kate shook her head. That wasn't good enough. She didn't just want to be safe when Will was around to protect her. She didn't want to have to rely on someone else to stay safe, even him. She wanted to be strong in her own right, and now there was a way.

"I could come with you," Will suggested.

"I think I need to do this alone," Kate said, because anything else would have meant explaining exactly what she intended. Even after everything Geoffrey had said, she still had a hard time believing that there might be a magic fountain that could make her unbeatable. Trying to explain that to Will would be even worse.

"At least try to be safe?" Will said, moving to stand close to her. Close enough that for a moment, Kate thought that he was going to kiss her. He didn't, though, and Kate found herself feeling a hint of disappointment at that.

Maybe when she got back.

"I will," Kate said. "And I'll be back soon, you'll see."

She would be. With the strength she got from the fountain, she would be able to do all the things she'd wanted.

The ride to the forest took longer than Kate expected. Her horse was strong and fast, but Kate wasn't enough of a rider to send it to the south at a full gallop. Instead, she rode at a steady pace, sticking to the broad, paved roads at the start, then pulling off onto dirt tracks as the trees came into view.

She tried to remember the map from the book. The spot marked on it had been specific, but she hadn't seen the map for long. There had been something about way markers, and a staircase. Kate just hoped that they would be obvious.

They were. She found the first of them before she reached the forest. It was a block of stone, designs on it worn almost smooth by time and weather. Kate's fingers traced a design that could have been a fountain, or could have been the maw of some great beast. There was an arrow cut into the stone, pointing to a smaller track. Kate took it.

Slowly, the foliage started to surround Kate, pressing in until she had to dismount and lead the horse. She didn't want to leave it, but the trail was getting narrow enough that she might have to if things kept going like this.

She caught a flash of worked stone by the trail, and it was such a contrast to the tangled branches that pulled at her that she stopped, looking at it more closely. Kate brushed away a tangle of ivy with her foot, and saw that beneath it there was the stone block of a step. Another stood above it, and another, in a set of stone steps that had been all but lost to time and moss.

Kate tied her horse off now, taking a knife from her saddlebags and the wooden sword that she'd made as a way to practice designing blades. She used the wooden blade to clear away some of the tangled foliage ahead of her, cutting with the knife whenever she needed a sharp edge.

Her hacking revealed more stone in the form of another way marker, this one almost as tall as she was. It had carved symbols on it, in the lines and swirls of a language that had nothing to do with the kingdom's. There was something else too: an image of a fountain.

Kate's breath caught at that, and she hurried up the rest of the steps, daring to hope that this might all be real. She'd been sure that this was all some story, and then that she wouldn't be able to find the fountain even if it did exist. Now, it seemed as though it might just be a short way away.

Kate's feet slipped and stumbled as she climbed the stone steps, moss giving way underneath her, while brambles that seemed solid as she grasped them proved to be anything but. She ended up leaning on her practice blade the way someone else might have used a walking stick, using it to test the ground ahead of her while she clambered up the crumbling steps. Each one seemed designed to challenge her as she made her way forward.

"I hope the fountain is worth it," Kate said as she climbed.

Although it wasn't that far, the climb was difficult enough that it took her long minutes to reach the top. When she did, there was another short path through even denser trees, which seemed to block out the light, turning the world into something strange and unknown. They tangled together to form a kind of leafy arch, and Kate stepped through it, into an open space on the other side.

There were no trees here, just more of the ancient stone she'd clambered up to get here. It stood in the ruins of something that seemed far older, with fragments of wall there sticking out of the turf like teeth, and broken columns seeming like fingers reaching up through the grass. All of them were the dilapidated relics of some far earlier time, before the civil wars, maybe before even the kingdom.

The fountain stood at the heart of it, and one glance at it made Kate's heart fall.

In another time, it might have been impressive. It was broad and dark, cut from local stone so finely that it seemed to be a natural extrusion from the landscape rather than a man-made structure. It was a broad shell shape, curling up with a statue standing at the center that might have been a woman once, but was now so covered in moss that it was hard to tell.

The fountain wasn't flowing anymore.

That fact, more that the rest of it, told Kate just how useless her journey now was. Crumbling stonework wasn't promising, but ultimately, it meant nothing. She'd come for a fountain, though. She'd assumed that there might be something special about the water there, something magical. Now that there was no water, it felt as though she'd let herself get carried away by what Geoffrey had told her. It felt stupid, to spend her time here rather than at the forge, crafting the sword that was currently only wooden.

Kate sat back against the fountain, closing her eyes to push back tears. She'd been so stupid to come here. Stupid to think that she could ever be as strong as the boys from Will's regiment. It had been an empty dream.

134

"Why would a fountain make someone strong?" Kate demanded of the forest around her.

"Fountains can't," a woman's voice said. "But if people are looking for a fountain, it makes it easier for me to find them."

Kate's eyes snapped open, and she stood, holding her wooden practice sword out in front of her. A woman stood there, wearing a hooded robe of deep, forest green. She had dark hair that appeared to be tangled with ivy, and eyes of a leaf green that seemed to match the plants around her. She was older than Kate, perhaps thirty, but with a look to her that said she might be even older than that.

"I've been threatened with many things before," the woman said. She pushed aside Kate's practice blade gently. "Never with a stick."

"I—" Kate lowered the weapon. "I'm sorry, you caught me by surprise."

"But you came to this place," she said. "You came looking for help, or you would not be here."

"I just didn't expect..." Kate began. She realized that she must sound like an idiot. "Who *are* you?"

Instinctively, Kate reached out to read the other woman's mind, but all that met her was something that felt as solid as a wall. Her attempt to get through just slid off it, and Kate stared at the other woman in shock.

"I am someone who is not so easily read by a gift such as yours," she replied, although she didn't seem angry at the intrusion. If anything, she seemed happy about it, which was the one reaction Kate hadn't expected. "And now you are wondering if we are the same. We are not the same, girl. Mine is a much darker version of your powers. And much more twisted. One you should beware to pry too deeply into."

Kate suddenly felt a flash of this woman's mind, as if sent to her, and she involuntarily raised her hands to her ears and shrieked. It was so dark, so awful, a blur of horrific images, all moving too fast to make out, but leaving an impression of incredible horror.

Finally, it stopped.

Kate removed her hands from her ears, breathing hard, staring wide-eyed. Never in her life had someone invaded her mind like that. She had all this time assumed she was impervious. That no one else's mind was more powerful than hers.

She looked this woman—if that's what she was—up and down with a new fear, and a new respect. Perhaps she shouldn't have come here after all.

135

The woman grinned in return, an ugly, invasive grin.

"Who are you?" Kate asked again.

The woman was silent for a long time. Finally, she spoke.

"Some call me Siobhan," she said. "But names are merely labels for the weak. You have come here for a reason. Ask for what it is you want, and I will tell you the price."

Kate blinked.

"I don't understand," Kate said.

The woman frowned, and Kate could guess at the disapproval there.

"Don't waste my time, girl. You came here for a reason. You were looking for something. What is it?"

Kate swallowed, but refused to allow herself to be cowed by Siobhan's tone. She would be strong.

"I want to be able to fight," she said. "I want to have enough power that I'm never helpless again."

The other woman stood there in silence for a few heartbeats. Kate could feel each one thudding against the inside of her chest. What would she do when the other woman said no? What would she do when Siobhan told her that it was impossible, and Kate was wasting her time?

"You have a talent, and I could teach you to build on it. I could teach you to fight in ways that have nothing to do with the crude strength of men. I could teach you to harness powers beyond anything you've seen."

She made it sound so simple, when her whole life, Kate had been told that there were some things that were too evil even to talk about. There was a reason Kate and Sophia had hidden what they could do.

"You wouldn't have to be afraid of what you are any longer," Siobhan said. "You could be strong. You could be *free*. My kind can help yours, if you let us."

A part of Kate wanted to say yes, but she knew better than to do that. People were rarely so generous.

"And what would *you* want?" Kate asked.

Siobhan seemed pleased. "In return, two things."

"*Two* things?" Kate retorted.

"You ask a great deal of me," the woman replied. "Two things does not seem unreasonable."

She made it sound almost playful, as though the whole thing was a game. There was something about the laugh that followed that almost didn't seem human. It seemed as though the forest itself was laughing.

136

"What things?" Kate asked, in spite of it.

"Apprentice to me and learn all I wish to teach you."

That didn't sound so different from the arrangement she had with Thomas. It didn't sound so different, in a lot of ways, to the best kind of arrangement that might have resulted from her indenture.

"And the second thing?" Kate asked.

The other woman stepped into the fountain, and for a moment, shimmered. Kate saw an image of it bright and new, filled with water. The statue above shone, and it looked far too similar to the witch there for Kate's taste.

There came a long silence. Then:

"A favor."

Kate cocked her head to one side. "*What* favor?"

Siobhan laughed that worrying laugh again. She seemed to be enjoying this whole thing far too much. "I haven't decided. But you would do it, whatever it was."

That was a much bigger thing to ask. Kate wasn't sure that she could stomach that.

She shook her head. It was too much. It was far too much. She sensed this woman's darkness, and she sensed that, whatever favor it was, it would be horrific. It would be like selling her soul.

She backed away from the fountain, one step at a time.

"No," she said, surprised to hear her own words, surprised to hear herself turn down the only thing she'd ever wanted.

The woman merely grinned in return, as if knowing Kate had no choice.

Kate backed away, and as soon as she reached the steps, she ran, stumbling as she went. Siobhan's mad laughter followed her.

"I'll be here when you change your mind."

137

CHAPTER TWENTY TWO

Sophia still couldn't believe that Sebastian had proposed to her. She'd barely been able to get used to the fact that she'd found a place in the palace as his lover, and now, suddenly, his ring sat on her finger. She couldn't believe that things had swept forward so quickly, and that she was now getting married. It felt like being carried along by a stream, so fast that there was no way to know what was happening half the time.

Sophia hadn't known that planning a wedding could involve so much. She had known that it wouldn't just be a question of finding a priest, when it came to royalty, but there were complexities that she had never considered. There were feasts to be organized, announcements to be made. There were even permissions to be sought, because the dowager and the Assembly of Nobles would have to give their blessing before a prince's marriage could go ahead. The latter, according to those officials she asked, would be a formality. This was one matter where the nobles would go along with whatever their ruler said.

Getting Sebastian's mother to agree sounded like anything but a formality. She had been kind enough during the dinner where Sophia had met her, but Sophia wasn't stupid enough to believe that a ruler would be happy about one of her sons marrying someone who couldn't cement an alliance or bring in new lands. Currently, Sophia found herself surrounded by a small coterie of helpers, with a clerk going through all the etiquette of asking permission, a dressmaker working on designs for a wedding gown, and the palace cook talking about whether they should have swan or goose.

"Obviously, it's the tradition *here*, but I thought that perhaps I could do a selection of delicacies from your home."

Their names flickered through the cook's mind, so Sophia picked a couple, then waved the issue away.

"I'm sure you'll make it wonderful, whichever you choose," Sophia said. She wished that Cora were there to help her navigate a route through it all.

She wished that Sebastian were there, rather than caught up in preparations for the army and the role he would have within it. Sophia felt as though there was only so much she could do alone and being with him... well, that was kind of the *point* of all this, wasn't it? What was the point of getting married if her husband-to-be wasn't even there?

If she were just doing this to have a good life, that might not have mattered. She could have designed the dream wedding, without the almost unnecessary presence of a husband. Sophia could imagine Angelica sitting quite happily in one of Sebastian's rooms, ordering around servants as she planned for her position as his wife.

Sophia wanted Sebastian. More than that, she loved him. She felt the ache of need whenever he wasn't there, and the world seemed to brighten whenever he was. Now, it seemed that she was trapped in the middle of preparations for a wedding, without the chance to actually see her husband-to-be.

Then he was there, and Sophia stood to throw her arms around him. She was shocked when he took a step back.

"Sebastian?"

"Come with me, Sophia," he said.

"What is this about?" Sophia asked. She tried to pick the answer from Sebastian's thoughts, but right then, those were a tangled mess, filled with hurt and confusion. There was too much in there at once to focus on any one strand. "Did something happen? Sebastian, what's going on?"

"I was hoping you could tell me that," Sebastian said, in a tone that made Sophia's blood seem to turn to ice. Something had gone wrong. The girls in the castle had invented a rumor about her, or his mother had refused the marriage. Maybe the shop to which she had sold the dress had come to tell Sebastian about his new bride. There were so many things that could have gone wrong with her plan that it always seemed as though it was held together only through gossamer strands.

Sophia didn't know which thing had gone wrong, so she followed Sebastian through the palace, moving from the main quarters to the guest rooms, going to one where everything seemed ordinary, except that a guard stood outside the door.

"Thank you," Sebastian said to the man. "You can go now."

"Yes, your highness," the man said. He walked off, but just his presence made Sophia wonder what was going on there.

When Sebastian pushed open the door, she had an answer of sorts. The room had been repurposed as an artist's studio, most of the furniture stripped away to make way for canvasses stretched out, ready for work. Sophia didn't have to ask whose quarters these were: they were obviously for Laurette van Klet, the artist Sebastian had brought in to create a portrait of Sophia. The sketches of Sophia said as much. Even the beginnings of a painting sat at the heart of it all, worked in oil. It wasn't anywhere near complete yet, and Sophia suspected that it was itself a preparatory piece for a bigger work, but it was still further along than she'd thought, showing her as she'd been in the garden, informal and more beautiful than she suspected she was in real life.

"Well?" Sebastian asked.

"Well, it's beautiful," Sophia said. "But I don't understand—"

"Here," Sebastian said, pointing to a spot on the painting. A spot where Sophia's dress had ridden up in the casual joy of the day, revealing a stretch of her calf, and the mark that sat there like an accusation.

She'd covered it up with makeup for the ball. She'd done it intermittently since, but she hadn't today. She'd forgotten. Had she forgotten for their trip along the river too? The truth was that she didn't know, but the evidence was right there in front of her. The only question was what she was going to do with it now.

"I don't understand," was all she could think to say.

Sebastian shook his head. "Don't lie to me, Sophia. Laurette paints what she sees. *Only* what she sees." He reached for her then, and although Sophia started to pull back, he caught her by the shoulders. "Some of the women around the palace have been talking too, saying that something seems wrong about you. I thought they were just being jealous, but what if they aren't?"

Sophia tried to stop him as he lifted the hem of her dress, knowing that once he did this was over. There was nothing she could do though, and in moments, the symbol of indenture tattooed onto her calf was plain to see.

Sebastian stared at it for several seconds, and then stepped back. Sophia could feel the shock rising from him, his thoughts coming in such a rush that it was hard to keep up with them all. She watched as he sank to the floor in the midst of the arranged easels, looking as though he were trying to shut out the world.

"Sebastian," Sophia began, wanting to go to him to comfort him, but that wouldn't work, would it? Not when she was the one hurting him.

He looked up, and Sophia could see the glimmer of tears in his eyes. It was something she hadn't expected, and something she had definitely never wanted to be the cause of.

"Why?" he demanded. "Why lie to me, Sophia? Is that even your real name?"

"Yes," Sophia assured him. For the first time since she'd met him, she let the accent she'd assumed fall. "Just not of Meinhalt."

140

"Even your voice isn't real?" Sebastian said, and now he sounded distraught. "We've known each other... what? Days, at best. We don't know anything about one another, do we? Who *are* you?"

Sophia swallowed at that question. It was one she wasn't sure she knew the answer to herself. She'd tried to create an answer, but it wasn't the real one. She asked herself the question over and over without an answer. It still hurt to hear it from Sebastian, though.

She wanted desperately to tell him everything. About herself, her past, and above all, about how much she genuinely loved him. About how, even if all else was fake, her love for him was real. About how she never meant to hurt him. How her lying, her behaving like this, wasn't even her.

But in her frenzy of emotions, the words caught in her throat. All she could manage was:

"I didn't want it to be like this."

Sebastian stood, going over to one of the canvasses. As sudden as a storm, he picked it up and smashed it, tearing through it.

"You tricked me!" he cried out. "You took advantage of me! All you were after was my wealth! My position! You never cared for me at all!"

She felt a pain in her chest at his words, at the sudden violence of it all, of seeing her image being torn to bits. It was a fitting image for how she felt about herself, her life, all being torn to bits about her.

Despite her best efforts, she started to cry. She stood there and cried like a little girl with no one to comfort her.

It seemed to surprise Sebastian. He stopped what he was doing, and his rage abated. He stared back at her, as if sorry, as if realizing he'd gone too far.

And yet he did not come to comfort her.

She wanted so badly to read his thoughts, and yet they were such a jumble of heightened emotions, of contradictory feelings, she could not read them at all.

"I don't have anywhere to go," Sophia involuntarily blurted out.

She immediately regretted it. She didn't want his sympathy anymore, or his help.

And yet still, he stood there, silent. His rage and shock seemed to be calming, his face seemed to be conforming to something like compassion, or pity.

She didn't want pity. And least of all from him.

She wanted love. True love. And she realized in that instant that, even if she'd found it with Sebastian, she'd lost it forever.

Sophia stepped back.

Wiping her flowing tears, she pulled off the ring that he'd given her. She let it fall to the carpet, because she didn't dare to touch Sebastian again and she couldn't take it with her.

She wanted so desperately to say: *I want you to know that, whatever else was a lie, my love was not.*

But at that moment, a sob rose in her throat, so great, it drowned out all speech.

All she could do was turn around and flee. Flee from this castle, this man she loved, and this life that lay just beyond the reach of her fingertips.

CHAPTER TWENTY THREE

Kate returned to Ashton in frustration, but also with a kind of peace. Frustration, because she hadn't gained the strength that she was looking for. Peace, because it made things simpler in a lot of ways. She couldn't take the witch's offer, and so her life would go back to straightforward days of being Thomas's apprentice at the forge, trying to learn about blades by swinging them at the air.

It wasn't what she'd wanted when she'd set off into the city, but it had the potential to be a good life, particularly with Will there. Maybe you didn't get what you wanted in life, but maybe the alternatives could still be good. The thought of Will waiting back at the forge made Kate smile as she came up to the outskirts of the city. It wouldn't be long before she was back now.

Kate dismounted, walking her horse on the last stretch toward the smithy. She'd ridden long enough for one day, her legs aching with the effort of it.

"When we get back," she told the horse, "you can have a quiet life again, and I'll be the best apprentice Thomas could ask for."

He was definitely a better teacher than the alternative. He was kind, and patient, and crucially, being a smith's apprentice presented no risk to owing a witch an unnamed favor. There were some things she couldn't do, even for the strength to be able to take revenge. Realizing that brought a kind of peace with it, as if a flame that had threatened to consume everything in Kate had dimmed.

Maybe that was a good thing, though. Maybe all of this was a sign that she should put aside violence. Maybe—

"There you are!" a voice called. "I know you!"

And Kate knew that voice. The last time she'd heard it, its owner had been chasing her to the edge of the river, determined to beat her to a pulp before dragging her back to the orphanage.

Sure enough, when she looked, the biggest of the boys from the docks was there, swaggering toward her with the certainty of someone who knew that there was nowhere for Kate to go. He took his time, and Kate knew enough about the tactics of bullies to know that he was just giving her time in which to be scared.

She could read from his thoughts that he could barely believe his luck at having found her at last after looking for so long.

143

He didn't look good. He still had bruises from the scuffle down on the docks, but they were matched by fresh marks that had clearly come from a beating. If it had been anyone else, Kate might have felt some sympathy for him. As it was, she edged away from him, wondering if she could get on the horse and ride clear.

"There's no point running," he said. "I've spent days looking for you, you little bitch! The others crawled back to the orphanage, said they'd rather be sold to a mine than keep looking. I kept going, though."

"Good for you," Kate shot back. She was still working her way toward the horse. If she could mount it, she could be away from this idiot as quickly as she had been on the river.

"Good for me, bad for you," the boy said. "*Don't* try to run. You think I don't know you're working for the smith? I looked for you. I asked about you. And now…"

Kate gave up edging toward the horse, holding her ground as the boy came forward.

"And now what?" Kate asked. "You don't have two friends to help you this time."

"You think I need them? To deal with one girl? I've hunted you, I've avoided the hunters myself, and now I'm going to make you beg me to drag you back."

Kate took the practice blade out of her belt. It was only wooden, but it was still long enough to threaten with.

"You need to think about this," Kate said.

"I am thinking," the boy said. "I'm thinking that when I bring you back, they'll let me join one of the hunting gangs. I'll pay my indenture with my first catch. I'll be able to do what I want, then."

Kate sighed at the stupidity of it all. She knew all about the way plans worked out in the real world. "You can *already* do what you want. Look, what's your name?"

"Zachariah," the boy said defensively, as if expecting some trick.

"Well, Zachariah, look at where you are. You aren't in the orphanage, are you? You aren't in the middle of being indentured. You can walk away and do what you want. You've avoided the hunters for a day or two, so why not forever? There aren't as many in the country, are there? You can just turn around and walk away."

It seemed so obvious to her. Neither one of them was indentured or in danger. The boy would go his way, she would go hers, and the House of the Unclaimed wouldn't have any hold over them. He might be able to forge a life out there, whether it was finding a farm to work on or, more likely, taking to a life of robbery. Wasn't that enough?

"I could," he said. "I don't want to. What I *want* to do is beat you bloody, yell for the watch, and then laugh while they drag you back. Guards!"

He shouted it loud enough that Kate winced.

"Guards! There's a runaway!" He looked at Kate with a sneer on his face. "And when they catch you, they'll make you give up that sister of yours. Maybe I'll get to—"

"Don't you talk about my sister!" Kate yelled, swinging the practice blade at his head. He flinched and it hit his shoulder, bouncing off.

"I'm going to beat you to a pulp," he promised, charging forward. He slammed into Kate, and in an instant the two of them were tumbling to the ground, the momentum of the rush carrying them both down together.

Kate hit at him with her wooden blade, but the boy caught it, twisting it from her hand. He hit her hard, and in that instant, Kate might have been back on the training ground, or by the dock. She tasted blood the same way, felt her head ringing. She felt the same sense of utter helplessness, and she *hated* it.

"I'm going to leave you looking as though you've been kicked by that horse of yours," he said. "Then I'm going to find your sister, and I'm going to drag you both back together."

Kate reached out for the wooden sword he'd knocked from her hand. He hit her again, then grabbed it himself, lifting it up.

"Oh, do you want this?" he demanded.

"No," she replied, and her voice sounded strange even to herself. "I just want your hands full."

She pulled her eating knife from its sheath and buried it in his chest in one movement.

It was easier than she'd thought it would be. The knife was sharp, and the boy's flesh was soft, but even so, it didn't feel as though it should be that easy to kill someone. It shouldn't be that simple to just slide a knife up under someone's ribs, listening to them gasp as it reached their heart.

Zachariah looked shocked by the sudden pain of it. He looked as though he was going to try to say something, maybe call for the watch again, but the words didn't come. Instead, blood trickled at the side of his mouth, and he slumped, his weight collapsing onto Kate.

The worst part was that her power let her see the moment when he died, his thoughts going from pain and panic to a kind of total

145

emptiness as his spirit fled him. She sensed the instant when he died, and she felt...

...well, what did she feel? That was a harder question than Kate had thought. That he'd deserved it, mostly. That she needed to get out from under the sheer dead weight of him before it crushed her. Not remorse though. Not yet. Not the panic that Kate was sure she ought to have felt, because she'd just *killed* someone.

Instead, she found herself feeling almost weirdly calm about it. Still, like the center of a storm, as if the rest of the world were something not really happening. Kate pushed her way free of the boy's greater bulk, wiping her knife clean and then seeing that there was blood on her tunic as well. There was nothing she could do about that, though.

In the distance, whistles and shouts signaled the approach of guardsmen, or just locals banding together when someone had called for help. That was what they did when there was danger, wasn't it? They sent up the cry and all those who lived there joined in to chase off thieves or fend off wolves. Or hang murderers. Kate heard them getting closer, and for the longest time, all she could do was stand there, trying to make sense of it.

Now, emotion started to creep in past the shock of it all. She'd just killed someone, and the full horror of that landed on her like a lead weight. Whatever the reason, whatever the situation, she'd just stabbed someone. If the watch came for her, or the rougher justice of the mob, would it make any difference that he'd been beating her half to death at the time?

Somehow, Kate doubted it. She went back to her horse, half stumbling with a combination of emotion and the pain of her beating. It took her three attempts just to mount it, pulling herself up into the saddle clumsily and almost falling even then.

She didn't know what to do with Zachariah's body, wasn't sure that she *could* do anything, when the sheer dead weight of him was so much to move. In any case, the sounds of trouble were coming closer, and there was no time. So she left him there, in the middle of the road, riding in the direction of the blacksmith's shop.

As Kate rode, the full implications of everything she'd just done started to sink in. She was one of the indentured, running away from her fate, who had killed someone when he tried to take her back. They would kill her for that, and it would be a miracle if they only hanged her for it, rather than leaving her in a gibbet to starve or breaking her on a wheel.

She was almost back to the smithy before she realized the truth: she couldn't go back. Kate didn't know if anyone had seen her fighting Zachariah. Certainly, someone would have heard what he was shouting. It wouldn't take much for people to work out that she was the one he'd found, especially if he'd been asking questions about her.

If she went back, she would lead trouble straight to Thomas and Winifred's door. Straight to Will. What was the penalty for aiding a murderer? Just the thought of something happening to Will made Kate feel sick.

He and Thomas were outside when Kate came back. She didn't dismount. She didn't dare, because if she dismounted, they might talk her into staying, or might tell her that they would protect her from what was coming when they couldn't. When no one could.

"Kate," Will said with a smile. "You're back! That's good, you're just in time, my father and I have a surprise for—"

"Will," his father said, cutting him off. Thomas obviously saw more than his son did. "Quiet a moment. Something's wrong."

Kate sat there on the horse, just staring at them, not knowing what to say. It seemed wrong to say anything, because the moment she did, she would bring a wealth of pain down onto the only people who had ever shown her kindness.

"Kate?" Will said. "What's happening? Why is there blood on your tunic? Did someone attack you?"

Kate nodded. "A boy from the House of the Unclaimed. He wanted to take me back. He attacked me and—" It was hard to come out and say it. She didn't want Will or Thomas thinking of her as some kind of monster.

"And?" Thomas asked.

"And I killed him," Kate said. "I didn't have a choice."

Was that true? It had seemed as though she hadn't had any other options when she'd plunged the knife in, but the truth was, by then, she'd *wanted* Zachariah dead. He'd deserved it, after all he'd done, and all he'd threatened to do.

"Get inside," Will said. "We'll need to hide you."

Thomas understood better, though. "They'd find her even if we hid her, Will. They'll know I have a new apprentice. It won't take them long."

"Then what do we do?" Will asked.

Kate answered that. "There's only one thing I can do: I have to leave. If I get away from the city, they won't look for me forever, but if I stay here, they'll hurt you as well as me."

"No," Will said. "We can stop it happening. We can fight them."

Kate shook her head then. "We can't. Not all of them. They'd just kill you alongside me, and I don't want that, Will. I have to go."

Kate could feel the pain and disappointment boiling off Will like smoke. It matched some of what she felt in that moment, but she knew he didn't understand the dangers that were coming.

"I don't want you to go," he said.

"And I don't want to go," Kate replied. "But I have to. I'm sorry, Will. Thomas, thank you, you gave me a home, and I wish I could have learned more."

"You would have been a good apprentice," Thomas said. "I have something for you. It was going to be a surprise for you. Will?"

Will didn't respond for a moment, but then nodded. He went to a spot where a cloth covered something, pulling it away. Kate saw the gleam of a sword. More than that, it was a sword she recognized, because she wore the wooden version of it on her hip.

"There wasn't enough time to do more than forge the basic blade," Thomas said. "I'd intended the sharpening, the handle wrap and the detail work to be part of your training, but it's strong, and it's light."

He took it and handed it up to Kate. It was a long way from finished, but it was still more than she could have expected. It was long and light, feeling as though it would be perfectly balanced once she wound a handle onto it. It was probably the most beautiful thing she'd ever owned.

"I worked on it with my father," Will said. "We wanted it to welcome you back. Now... I guess it's a going away present."

"I don't know what to say," she said. "Thank you. Thank you both so much."

Kate took it, settling it into place next to the wooden blade so that the two of them hung side by side from her belt. She felt as though she ought to say something more than just thank you. There was so much more she *wanted* to say, so much she wanted to do, but she could still hear the shouts in the distance, escalating as they found the body she'd left behind. Those made it clear that there wasn't enough time for anything else.

She had to settle for leaning down from the saddle, kissing Will quickly and sharply, not even sure if she was doing it right. It wasn't as though she'd had any time to practice kissing. She straightened up before he could say anything, although that didn't make much of a difference when her talent told her all of the things that he wanted to say anyway. Even hearing them like that hurt,

148

making it feel as though turning would tear her heart out of her chest.

Kate did it anyway. She put her heels to the horse and rode away, listening for the shouts that were building as more people started to search for her. She didn't have to think about where she was going. There was only one place she *could* go, if she wanted to survive.

It seemed that the woman at the fountain would be getting what she wanted after all.

CHAPTER TWENTY FOUR

Sophia walked the streets of Ashton, and this time it was worse than it had been before. The last time, she had been fresh out of the orphanage, just grateful to get away from it. She'd also had her sister beside her, and between the two of them, it had seemed that anything was possible.

Now, though, it just hurt with the sense of loss that had been there ever since Sebastian had told her that she had to go. It didn't matter that he didn't want this any more than she did. What mattered was that he'd said it. He'd turned her out onto the street as surely as his brother would have after he'd gotten what he wanted. He'd said it was to protect Sophia, but wasn't it really just as much to protect himself? Wasn't he really just worried about what would happen when his mother or the other nobles found out who he'd fallen in love with?

Sophia felt the heat of the tears falling as she walked, and didn't even try to hold them back. No one looked her way as she kept going along the cobbled streets of one of Ashton's wealthier quarters. Nobody stared at her broken-hearted wandering. Nobody cared enough to look.

Kate! she sent for the millionth time. *Where are you?!*

And yet no answer came.

For the first time in her life, Sophia felt truly alone.

Being on the street was worse this time because of everything she'd almost had. Sophia had felt as though she'd been on the verge of everything she could have wanted: a safe life with a man she loved and who seemed to love her back; a place among the wealthiest nobles of the realm; acceptance as something more than just an orphan, suitable only for indenture as whatever the ones who purchased her debt chose.

Sophia kept going, not wanting to stop where she might be seen and recognized. It was embarrassing enough that this had happened at all, without thinking about what might happen if someone from the palace spotted her. She didn't want to think about how Milady d'Angelica would gloat if she found out that Sophia had been forced to leave the palace, her wedding canceled.

She really didn't want to think about what might happen if she found out the truth. What would happen if the noble girl realized that she'd been tricked, beaten to the love of the prince by a girl who was just one of the indentured?

What would Sebastian say had happened? That she'd been called back to her adopted country? That there had been some unnamed scandal? Would Sebastian say anything at all? Perhaps the dowager would let it be known that even mentioning Sophia of Meinhalt would incur her displeasure, and that would be that.

Whatever happened, Sophia wouldn't be able to go back, and that made it worse too. When she'd first left the orphanage, there had been a glimmer of hope left in her dream of finding a place among the nobles. Now, Sophia felt as though she had spent the last of her hope, with nothing left but the prospect of a worse life to come.

At least she wouldn't be sleeping with her back to a chimney tonight. She still had the money that she'd gotten by selling her stolen dress. She could buy... well, if she was careful, Sophia could buy a lot of things, but right then it hurt too much to think about all the things that might happen next. She just wanted a room for the night so that she could sleep and weep away the pain of being pushed out of Sebastian's life.

Could she have done anything differently? Sophia asked herself the question again and again as she looked around, searching for an inn that might still have a room left for her. There didn't seem to be a good answer to that. She could have done a better job of disguising her mark, obviously, but the truth was that no matter how careful she'd been, sooner or later, someone would have seen it. It was there, indelibly labeling her as something lesser; something to be hated. She would have forgotten the makeup another time, or it would have washed off in the rain, and then...

Well, maybe then it wouldn't have been when Sebastian was the only one to see. Maybe a dozen nobles would have been there to grab her and demand her life for the insult of it, rather than there just being one man who cared about her.

Sophia went on until she found an inn away from the palace. She wanted to be far enough from the noble district that she wouldn't be recognized by any of the nobles there or their servants, but she didn't want to go all the way down into the worst parts of the city. There were some places that she didn't want to return to, even if it would cost her an extra coin or two to stay here.

She walked in, trying to keep from showing too much of the hurt that cut through her heart, making her feel as though she should simply keep walking until she dropped from exhaustion. The inn was a long way from the luxury of the palace, but it seemed to be clean, and the people staying there seemed more like merchants passing through the city than rough dock hands or mercenaries.

Sophia didn't feel safe there, because where *could* she be safe when she'd even found herself in danger in the palace? Even so, it would be good enough for tonight. After that... well, Sophia couldn't think past that. Maybe she would live her life as a thief, using her power to sense when people weren't looking until she was finally caught. Maybe she would try to find her sister, although Sophia hated the idea of bringing her troubles into whatever life Kate had found for herself.

She walked up to the bar of the inn, waiting for the attention of the innkeeper and taking out a couple of coins.

"I'd like a room for the night," she said. It was hard to say even that much without breaking down into sobs.

The innkeeper shook his head firmly. "We don't have any rooms left."

"But—"

"We don't have any rooms left," the man repeated, and this time, Sophia caught a hint of the thoughts behind it.

Coming in off the street with no baggage and sounding as though she's from the slums. Does she think I don't know a whore when I see one? If I have to throw her out face first, though, it won't look good.

The thoughts of everyone else there told her that they were thinking more or less the same thing. To them there was no way she could be anything other than some rich man's castoff.

Maybe that was even what she was, in a way.

"I'll have to find somewhere else then," Sophia said, trying to turn around with what she hoped was some shred of dignity. She made it to the door before the tears came back, and she stepped back out into the street, hoping that the growing darkness would hide from the world just how upset she was.

Every step hurt now, a sense of pointlessness and worthlessness cutting through everything Sophia did. She hadn't been able to find a place in the palace. She hadn't had the sense to go with her sister. She couldn't even find an inn that would take her. She didn't know what she was going to do next.

Sophia started to walk down toward the river, into the poorer parts of the city. She wasn't sure then why she was doing it, whether it was to find a cheaper inn where they might not care what she seemed to be, to simply keep walking, or to throw herself into the river's cold embrace. Right then, all three seemed equally likely, and Sophia wasn't sure that she cared about the difference.

She kept going, down into the narrower streets where the houses crowded together and there wasn't the same sense of the buildings being kept in good repair. She walked past figures in alleys without looking at them, and ignored a bawdy offer shouted at her from a doorway.

She was so hurt right then that she was numb to it all, the city turning into background noise to the crushing weight around her heart. Sophia took step after shuffling step, not caring about the sounds of Ashton as its nighttime denizens woke and came onto the streets.

Perhaps that numbness was why she didn't hear the footsteps following behind her at first. It was certainly why she didn't stretch out her talent to pick up the thoughts of those around her. She had enough problems with her own thoughts right then, without adding more men wondering if they could buy her for the evening, or thugs wondering whether they should fight someone.

It was only as she kept going that the truth came to her: someone was following her.

CHAPTER TWENTY FIVE

Kate rode away from the only happiness she'd ever been able to find, forcing herself not to cry. She rode faster than she had all day, ignoring the part where it was getting dark now and letting her horse simply run.

She had to run, because she was an outlaw now. She'd killed someone. She'd stolen this horse. Anyone hunting her would be trying to cut her throat or drag her to a gallows now, not bring her back to the House of the Unclaimed.

There had been the shouts of pursuit somewhere behind Kate when she first left. Those had faded into silence now, and Kate just had to hope that it wasn't because they were taking their anger out on Will and his family. By leaving, she hoped that she'd made it look as though she was betraying them along with everyone else, and that trouble would follow her, not them.

She rode until it was too dark to keep going, and the road was just a difference in the reflection of the moonlight. Even her horse was shying away from continuing, pulling toward the side of the road as it slowed. Kate took the hint, pulling fifty paces from the road before tying her horse to the branches of a low shrub and pulling the saddle from its back.

She slept on the rough ground, cold because she couldn't risk a fire, with the sword Thomas had given her set beside her on the ground in case someone came. She didn't know what she would do with it if they did. Would she kill them, the way that she'd killed the boy who'd tried to take her back? Would she be able to drive them off if she didn't?

Kate slept fitfully, unable to keep her eyes closed for long. Fears drifted together with nightmares, until she could barely tell which was which. Was she running from shadows in a house on fire, or were there actually people out there coming for her? Kate snapped awake a dozen times, sitting up with her breath coming fast, only to realize that the attackers coming at her were fragments of dreams.

It wasn't until the sun came up that she saw her horse had pulled free of the bush where she'd tied it. It was gone, tracks leading away into the distance. Kate walked in a wide circle, trying to find it, but it was gone. Maybe it had run off to live wild. Maybe it had gone back to the owner she had stolen it from.

Either way, it meant that she had to walk. Kate took the saddle bags, her sword, and the few other possessions that she had and then set off on foot. She didn't know if hunters would be coming after her now, but she went a different way from the hoof prints at first, keeping to stony ground where she wouldn't leave footprints, simply to make sure that anyone trying to track her would go in the wrong direction. Only once she was well clear of the spot where she'd camped did Kate set off back in the direction of the forest.

She kept off the road while she walked, moving instead between the edges of fields and the small tracks that meandered alongside the real roads. It meant that there was less chance of her being seen by someone who might know what she'd done, but it also meant that the sun was high before Kate saw the trees growing closer. She was tired by then, and hungry; she'd only slaked her thirst by drinking rainwater collected in the hollow of a low stone.

Kate was glad that things were going better for her sister than for her. Maybe they were two sides of a scale, so that as things went downhill for Kate, Sophia's life got better. Briefly, Kate thought of what might happen if she headed for the palace, asking Sophia for help. If she was that close to a prince, maybe she could secure some kind of pardon for Kate for all she'd done.

Kate laughed at that thought, continuing to head into the trees. If she showed up at the palace, they would turn her away at best, hang her at worst. There was only one direction she could go in now, and she was already going that way.

Kate headed into the trees, looking for the start of the stone staircase that led up to the fountain. Kate had considered every other possibility, but the truth was that there *weren't* any real options. She'd destroyed all of that the moment her eating knife had slid under Zachariah's ribs. Maybe she'd been heading for this from the moment she and Sophia had fled from the orphanage, caught by fate as surely as she would have been by any indenture.

Kate didn't want to believe that, but she was still walking toward the spot where the fountain waited for her, and Siobhan with it.

At least, she assumed that she was. Here in the forest, it was hard to tell which way she was going. The trees crowded in around her, pushing Kate back and forcing her further off the path with every step. This wasn't the way she'd come the first time she was here, and now the mud stuck to her boots, bogging her down while the branches scratched at her almost as if they were guarding the place.

Kate felt a flicker of amusement from up ahead. She straightened and listened. There came no sound, but that feeling had been unmistakable. The witch. She was here. Watching her. Taking pleasure in her suffering.

She was getting close.

Rain started to fall, hammering down through the trees and plastering Kate's clothes to her skin.

"I know what you're doing," Kate called out. "Let me through, damn you!"

There came no answer.

Yet even so, her way seemed to ease.

Thorns still pricked at Kate, but they didn't tangle and stop her. Mud still sucked at her feet, but it didn't threaten to pull her boots away. The trees didn't block the way now, but seemed to funnel her instead.

Finally, she found a small path that looked familiar. She'd been here yesterday; she was sure of it. She could see the crumbling stone of the first steps.

She looked up and braced herself.

And then, one step at a time, she started to climb.

CHAPTER TWENTY SIX

Sophia glanced back over her shoulder, trying to catch sight of the people following her. Still, she saw nothing.

Inside, her fear built, forcing her onward. She turned down a side street and the footsteps still kept in time with hers, and she paid them more attention. They followed the rhythm of her own steps, speeding up as she did, falling more softly as she looked around for threats. There were too many thoughts around in the city to be certain about who was following her or why, but she felt certain that there were at least three sets of thoughts close behind her.

She walked faster, and the footsteps sped up with her.

She broke into a run. She chose directions at random, heading through the gathering dark without caring about where she was going. She pulled into a courtyard, ducking through a half-open door and trying to calm her breathing enough that it wouldn't give her away. Carefully, so slowly that it was barely perceptible, Sophia closed the door the rest of the way. She wanted to leave no trace of her presence.

She stood there in the shadows, hoping that whoever was following would move on by, leaving her alone the moment she became too much trouble. That was the way predators worked in the city. They only hunted for what was easy, and left anything more difficult well alone. If she could stay quiet and out of sight, then they would move past her and look for another target somewhere else.

Then she caught a flicker of their thoughts and knew that wouldn't work. She backed away from the entrance, looking around for a weapon, but there wasn't anything, and in any case, Sophia wasn't her sister. She didn't have the ability to fight off attackers. She could talk to them, persuade them, run from them, but not fight them.

Sophia found herself looking for a way out, saw a stack of boxes on the far side of the courtyard, and started to climb. They didn't reach all the way to the sloping tiles of the roof, but they got close enough. She'd clambered over the roofs of the city before; she could do it again. She felt the roughness of the wooden boxes under her hands as she forced herself up from box to box, trying to work out a route to the tiled roof above. When she heard the door to the courtyard open, Sophia tried to move faster.

She felt the boxes shift beneath her, and then, in an instant, Sophia was falling.

She felt the impact of the cobbles below slam through her as she struck the floor, and Sophia couldn't even scream with the pain as the force of it knocked all the breath out of her. There were hands on her then, and Sophia thrashed around, trying to get free. It didn't make any difference.

Cloth came down over Sophia's face, shutting out the little light that there was, making it hard to breathe. Hands clamped down, and now Sophia *couldn't* breathe. She continued to fight, but she could feel the strength fading out of her, and blackness that had nothing to do with the cloth started to creep in around the edge of her vision.

A voice came to her, seemingly from a long way away.

"Did you really think you could escape the Masked Goddess?"

CHAPTER TWENTY SEVEN

Kate climbed and climbed, and this time, the steps seemed endless. She had the feeling she was being punished, tested. Perhaps she was just being reminded that she was something different from Siobhan, something less.

She kept going in spite of it, forcing herself upward.

By the time she reached the top, she felt ready to collapse. She approached the fountain, and right then, she found herself wishing that it was full, so that she could drink cool water from it.

Siobhan was standing beside it, looking elegant and untouched by the rain. She smiled, and there was cruelty there.

She stood there, staring at Kate in silence, her eyes burning through her.

Clearly, she would wait for Kate to speak first.

"I... I have nowhere else to go," Kate finally said, bowing her head, shame filling her.

Still, Siobhan waited, clearly wanting more.

Kate took a deep breath.

"I killed someone," she added. "They were going to take me back to the orphanage, and I killed them."

She saw the other woman nod with understanding.

"Lessons learned in blood are always the hardest ones," she finally said. "But they are the strongest too."

Siobhan reached out a hand.

The touch of her skin was as soft as moss or the brush of silk.

"You've learned what they will do to you out in the world. You have learned why you need to be strong."

Kate found herself nodding. She *did* need to be strong. She needed to be so strong that no one could hurt her again, and none of those hunting her could touch her. So that she could protect her sister. So that she could get her revenge on a childhood beaten out of her.

She needed more than that, though. She needed a place where she could be safe.

Siobhan walked to the far side of the fountain. The scene flickered, and Kate was looking at flowing water.

The fountain was alive again.

159

Kate was impressed by the woman's power. Yet she feared the waters before her, knowing the price they entailed.

Siobhan reached down with a small, silver ladle, and filled it with a steady hand.

She then turned to Kate, holding it out.

"Are you ready, Kate?"

Kate reached out with a trembling hand and took the ladle. It felt incredibly heavy in her hand, ancient, a thing in itself of great power.

She looked down at the shimmering waters inside it, and was surprised at how little water it held. Less than a small bowl.

Yet enough to change her life forever.

Enough to make her the strongest warrior that ever lived.

And enough to put her into this witch's debt forever.

It was not a pact she'd wanted to make.

Yet this was a hard, cruel world, and Kate, she realized, could rely on no one but herself.

She wanted that power. She wanted that strength.

She wanted to destroy that orphanage.

And she wanted to become the greatest warrior that ever lived.

So with a shaking hand, she raised the ladle to her lips, the metal cool, the water cooler.

And she closed her eyes.

And drank.

A COURT FOR THIEVES
(A Throne for Sisters—Book Two)

"Morgan Rice has come up with what promises to be another brilliant series, immersing us in a fantasy of valor, honor, courage, magic and faith in your destiny. Morgan has managed again to produce a strong set of characters that make us cheer for them on every page....Recommended for the permanent library of all readers that love a well-written fantasy."
--Books and Movie Reviews, Roberto Mattos (regarding Rise of the Dragons)

From #1 Bestseller Morgan Rice comes an unforgettable new fantasy series.

In A COURT FOR THIEVES (A Throne for Sisters—Book Two), Sophia, 17, finds her world upside down as she is cast from the romantic world of aristocracy and back to the horrors of the orphanage. This time the nuns seem intent on killing her. Yet that doesn't pain her as much as her broken heart. Will Sebastian realize his mistake and come back for her?

Her younger sister Kate, 15, embarks on her training with the witch, coming of age under her auspices, mastering the sword, gaining more power than she ever imagined possible—and determined to embark on a quest to save her sister. She finds herself immersed in a world of violence and combat, of a magic she craves—and yet one that may consume her.

A secret is revealed about Sophia and Kate's lost parents, and all may not be what it seems for the sisters. Fate, indeed, may be turned on its head.

A COURT FOR THIEVES (A Throne for Sisters—Book Two) is the second book in a dazzling new fantasy series rife with love, heartbreak, tragedy, action, adventure, magic, sorcery, dragons, fate and heart-pounding suspense. A page turner, it is filled with characters that will make you fall in love, and a world you will never forget.

Book #3 in the series—A SONG FOR ORPHANS—will be released soon.

"An action packed fantasy sure to please fans of Morgan Rice's previous novels, along with fans of works such as The Inheritance Cycle by Christopher Paolini.... Fans of Young Adult Fiction will devour this latest work by Rice and beg for more."

--The Wanderer, A Literary Journal (regarding Rise of the Dragons)

Books by Morgan Rice

THE WAY OF STEEL
ONLY THE WORTHY (Book #1)

A THRONE FOR SISTERS
A THRONE FOR SISTERS (Book #1)
A COURT FOR THIEVES (Book #2)
A SONG FOR ORPHANS (Book #3)

OF CROWNS AND GLORY
SLAVE, WARRIOR, QUEEN (Book #1)
ROGUE, PRISONER, PRINCESS (Book #2)
KNIGHT, HEIR, PRINCE (Book #3)
REBEL, PAWN, KING (Book #4)
SOLDIER, BROTHER, SORCERER (Book #5)
HERO, TRAITOR, DAUGHTER (Book #6)
RULER, RIVAL, EXILE (Book #7)
VICTOR, VANQUISHED, SON (Book #8)

KINGS AND SORCERERS
RISE OF THE DRAGONS (Book #1)
RISE OF THE VALIANT (Book #2)
THE WEIGHT OF HONOR (Book #3)
A FORGE OF VALOR (Book #4)
A REALM OF SHADOWS (Book #5)
NIGHT OF THE BOLD (Book #6)

THE SORCERER'S RING
A QUEST OF HEROES (Book #1)
A MARCH OF KINGS (Book #2)
A FATE OF DRAGONS (Book #3)
A CRY OF HONOR (Book #4)
A VOW OF GLORY (Book #5)
A CHARGE OF VALOR (Book #6)
A RITE OF SWORDS (Book #7)
A GRANT OF ARMS (Book #8)
A SKY OF SPELLS (Book #9)
A SEA OF SHIELDS (Book #10)
A REIGN OF STEEL (Book #11)
A LAND OF FIRE (Book #12)
A RULE OF QUEENS (Book #13)

About Morgan Rice

Morgan Rice is the #1 bestselling and USA Today bestselling author of the epic fantasy series THE SORCERER'S RING, comprising seventeen books; of the #1 bestselling series THE VAMPIRE JOURNALS, comprising twelve books; of the #1 bestselling series THE SURVIVAL TRILOGY, a post-apocalyptic thriller comprising three books; of the epic fantasy series KINGS AND SORCERERS, comprising six books; of the epic fantasy series OF CROWNS AND GLORY, comprising 8 books; and of the new epic fantasy series A THRONE FOR SISTERS. Morgan's books are available in audio and print editions, and translations are available in over 25 languages.

Morgan loves to hear from you, so please feel free to visit www.morganricebooks.com to join the email list, receive a free book, receive free giveaways, download the free app, get the latest exclusive news, connect on Facebook and Twitter, and stay in touch!

CPSIA information can be obtained
at www.ICGtesting.com
Printed in the USA
LVHW080517211220
674741LV00039B/517